DORIAN ROCKWOOD

THE DUNGEON OF PERIL MYSTERY

THE DUNGEON OF PERIL MYSTERY

For information contact:

Insundry Productions Books, Gardnerville NV 89460

insundryproductions.com

Cover illustration by Duy Phan

ISBN (ebook): 978-1-962056-07-6

ISBN (paperback): 978-1-962056-08-3

Library of Congress Control Number: 2025904266

Also By Dorian Rockwood
Treachery Unmasked

The Case Twins Adventures:
The Cash Cache Mystery
The Silent Witness Mystery

Chapter One

Seventeen-year-old Paul Case turned to his brother. "I hate you."

Dan grinned as he braked their war surplus jeep to a stop at a traffic light. "That was our bet, buddy. If you lost the boxing match to Jake, you'd model for my life drawing class."

"Don't remind me," Paul snapped.

"It was your defense that got you into this mess." Dan cocked an eyebrow at his twin. "If you wanted to keep your clothes on and not model, you should've blocked Jake's right cross."

"It was a split decision!" Paul argued.

"That was part of the wager." Dan pulled away from the intersection. The jeep jerked as he shifted into second gear. "Remember, I have a witness. Jake was standing next to us."

"It was my cornerman's fault." Paul glared at Dan.

"Hey, I was your cornerman for that fight. I said 'dig deep,' not 'hit the mat'," Dan said.

"Hardy-har-har, very funny." Paul crossed his arms over his chest as if shielding himself from the impending embarrassment. "I can't believe I'm going to stand on a box while a bunch of strangers scrutinize every muscle twitch."

"You've posed for me before," Dan said.

"Yeah, but that's different. You're only my dumb brother," Paul grumbled.

Dan laughed as he turned onto the street leading to the school's parking lot. "Come on, you're not stripping... I mean, not all the way. It's just, well, seminude, that's all."

Paul snorted. "Well, it's that 'nude' part that makes all the difference. Semi or not."

"Think of it this way. You'll be wearing what you do when you step into the ring," Dan said. "Or when we go swimming at the lake with Donna and Betty. Almost. Maybe less material..."

"Maybe less material..." Paul mimicked. He jabbed his finger at his sibling. "Danny boy, I swear, if even one person snickers one bit when I drop the robe, I'm going to start throwing punches."

"Don't worry. They won't," Dan said. "Besides, you might even have fun."

"Oh, yeah? Well, define 'fun,' there, pal," Paul shot back.

Dan grinned. He knew the athlete within his brother was unwilling to back down from a challenge — even one that involved less punching and more posing. "Trust me, you're already a step up from the last model."

"Who did you supposed artists draw before?" Paul asked.

"Not who, my dear brother, but what. Last week it was a stuffed raccoon. Posed with an apple. It was quite... avant-garde. Arty."

Dan turned into the school's driveway, the jeep bouncing over the curb cut leading to the parking area in the rear. Paul held onto the windshield to avoid getting pitched out.

"A stuffed raccoon?" Paul blinked. His face broke into an incredulous grin. "Okay, I guess being better than a dead animal stuffed with sawdust is something. Although it isn't exactly a high bar. Still, it's nice to know I won't be the worst model you've ever had."

The Belmont Adult Education Center was once an elementary school, built back in 1885, but now in 1948, it was a throwback to days gone by with its charming, outdated brick facade. The parking lot, in the past a bustling playground for young children, was now a faded asphalt canvas marked with remnants of childhood recess — circles, four-square courts, and hopscotch squares. Weather-worn basketball hoops still stood tall, their peeling paint a testament to countless games played. When the blacktop overflowed with vehicles, cars parked on the grassy field. Dan wheeled the jeep into a spot next to an old tether ball pole and switched off the engine.

"Let the unveiling commence," Paul said with a sigh. He jumped out of the passenger side and squared his shoulders.

Dan climbed out and went to his sibling. "Thanks for doing this, buddy. You're the best."

Paul ruffled Dan's brown hair and spoke like he was cooing to an infant. "Anything for my little baby brother."

Dan held up two fingers. "Younger only by two only minutes."

"Still counts." Paul pulled his gym bag off the floor under the back seat.

Dan smoothed his hair back into place. "Now go on, show them what the Case twins are made of. Just, you know, not too much of what we're made of. This is an art class, not anatomy."

Paul rolled his eyes.

"Remember, it's for the benefit of art," Dan said as he opened the metal toolbox the brothers used to carry things in the jeep. Out came his battered leather satchel, which held his supplies.

"Yeah, yeah, right, art," Paul echoed with mock enthusiasm. "I could inspire someone to paint a boxing match where the fighter actually keeps his clothes on."

"Hey, smile, my dear brother." Dan chuckled as the two started walking toward the school. He slapped Paul on his back. "You're about to be immortalized in charcoal and graphite. Think about it! You'll be posted on refrigerator doors all through the area! Belmont's own pinup! Here's an idea. Perhaps Mom will send the drawing out with our Christmas cards!"

Paul shot him a dirty look.

"And keep in mind, you're getting paid for it," Dan went on. "That's gotta take the sting out of stripping off your clothes in public, right?"

"*Some* of my clothes," Paul stressed. "You sure can sell it, buddy. But seriously, what kind of budget does this class have for models?"

"Enough to afford your rippling biceps and chiseled chest," Dan said. "You may be able to stop mowing lawns to earn money and go into modeling!"

"No, thank you." Paul shook his head emphatically. "At least in landscaping, I'm not watched every second while I work. Well, except for picky Mrs. Carmichael."

The early spring evening hugged the world in a pleasant but cool embrace. The air carried a lingering reminder of winter's chill, refusing to surrender fully to the warmth of the new season. A full moon, round and luminous, illuminated each detail of the scene before them. Its light cast long shadows from the trees and created an ethereal glow throughout the night.

Dan pulled open the building's weathered, heavy door with a loud scrape and the brothers stepped inside. Adults of all ages, including a few other high school students, moved up and down the corridor. Their size was a comic contrast to the drinking fountains fixed low on the wall for the school's previous pupils.

Paul stopped outside a glass showcase and pointed at a drawing of a fierce bear. "This is one of yours, isn't it?"

Dan gazed at the work with pride. "Yeah. I did it about three weeks ago."

"You have excellent control of line weight and variation. The hatching and cross-hatching add depth and texture," Paul chuckled at Dan's surprised expression. "See? I do listen to you when blabber about art." He smirked. "Sometimes."

They entered a classroom. The musty scent of crayons and bygone snack times seemed to linger in the air along with the pint-sized sink and low coat hooks of the former kindergarten. An "X-Y-Z" section of an alphabet border still clung tenaciously over the blackboard, and a faded rainbow mural remained on one wall.

Miss Cohen, the vivacious instructor, strode up to Dan and Paul. "Dan! This must be your brother."

"Yes, Miss Cohen," Dan gestured to his twin. "This is Paul."

Miss Cohen shook his hand. "Glad to meet you, Paul. Dan talks about you quite a bit." She took a step back to look at them. "My, you two are identical!"

Paul jerked his head toward Dan. "Except he doesn't wear glasses."

Dan copied the move in the opposite direction. "And he's a southpaw."

"Thank you for agreeing to pose for us tonight," the art teacher said.

"My pleasure. I've been looking forward to it," Paul smiled.

Dan choked down a derisive hoot.

"You'll find what you will wear is back there. It should fit." Miss Cohen indicated a curtained booth in the corner of the room next to a cubby filled with art supplies. "Come out when you've changed."

Paul sauntered behind the curtain as Dan moved to his easel and set up his pencils and charcoal the way he preferred. The other assorted students—two young college girls flipping through their sketchbooks, several middle-aged women chattering about shading techniques, and one grumpy man who appeared more interested in his newspaper than the prospect of a live model—were absorbed in their own pre-class rituals. After he finished, Dan went to the booth.

"Paul," Dan whispered through the curtain, "Are you ready yet?"

"What do you mean by 'ready'?" came the muffled reply.

"Ready as in not hiding in there until it's time for everyone to go home." Dan peeked inside the curtained space.

Paul stood there, wearing the briefest pair of white shorts Dan had ever seen. Paul gestured toward the skimpy garment and threw a poisonous look at Dan. "I hate you."

"We've already established that fact." Dan waved his brother out of the booth. "Come on, buddy, you look great. You'll knock them dead, tiger."

"Alright, let's get this bout done," Paul said at last, with a sigh of resignation.

"Just think majestic thoughts... like a stuffed raccoon," Dan threw over his shoulder as he left.

"I'll stuff you," Paul grumbled under his breath. As his brother returned to his easel, Paul stepped out from behind the curtain. He must have decided the best defense was a strong offense, so he strode toward the front of the room with the dramatic flair of an actor taking center stage. The women in the class, particularly the two young college girls, exchanged appreciative murmurers and glances as they took in Paul's athletic build.

Dan gave out a low wolf's whistle as Paul passed his easel.

"Shut up," Paul said out of the corner of his mouth.

"Remember, people, we're here to capture the essence of the human form, not rate it on a scale of one to ten," Miss Cohen reminded the students with a wink. "Although," she added in a stage whisper that carried through the room, "if we were rating, I'd say our model is far better than last week's."

Laughter bubbled up from the students, and even the grumpy man looked up from his paper to offer a begrudging nod of assent. Paul stood up to his full height of six feet, the artists' gaze turning him from reluctant participant to proud exhibit.

Dan chuckled to himself. His brother loved this. He knew he would.

"Now, as to pose…" Miss Cohen wondered.

"Michelangelo's David!" one of the middle-aged women gushed out in a breathless tone.

Miss Cohen nodded in agreement. She went to a small bookcase and pulled out a volume. Flipping through the pages, she went over to Paul. She showed him an image. Paul took off his glasses, and, after a few glances at the book and adjusting his position, struck a pose similar to the famous statue.

The room fell into silence for a second. Then the air was filled with a symphony of pencils and charcoals scratching onto drawing pads. Miss Cohen drifted from student to student, quietly making comments and suggestions.

With his hand moving fluidly across the page, Dan's strokes were precise and purposeful as he brought his brother's features to life on the paper. As usual, when he worked, Dan lost himself in the process, completely immersed in the rhythm of his work as his eyes, mind, and hand blended into one connected unit.

Dan was so engrossed, he was surprised when he heard Miss Cohen announce time was up for the evening. "That's all for tonight.

Let's all thank Paul for his modeling." She led a brief round of applause as Paul grinned.

With the final strokes of charcoal and a buzz of conversations signaling the end of class, Dan shuffled his sketches into a neat pile. He glanced around the room — easels stood like silent sentinels, their papers adorned with various interpretations of the human form, all inspired by Paul's stint as a seminude David.

Dan went up to his brother, now the object of attention of the two college girls. Their giggles filled the air, a melodic backdrop to Paul's animated recounting of a dramatic boxing match. He was claiming his footwork was better than the dancing skills of movie star Fred Astaire. "Hey Michelangelo, you can get dressed now."

"There's no rush." Paul returned a sly grin, shooing Dan away. He made no move to leave the conversation, clearly enjoying being the focus of the young women.

Dan rolled his eyes and went back to his easel to put away the rest of his art supplies.

"Paul," Miss Cohen's voice cut through the chatter as she approached him, envelope in hand. She extended the payment toward him. "For your outstanding contribution to the arts today. The class found it most helpful."

The girls giggled.

"Thanks. My pleasure." Paul took the envelope and gave it a light pat, as though confirming its contents by touch alone. The college students waved goodbye and departed, leaving behind an echo of their laughter.

"Dan," Miss Cohen began again, "Have you heard of Mrs. Margaret Maitland?"

Dan shook his head.

"Her husband founded the Belmont Foundry and owned it up to a few years ago. It secured many government contracts during the war and made quite a bit of money," Miss Cohen explained. "She lives in a mansion outside the city, on the banks of the river."

"Okay..." Dan didn't understand where this was all leading.

"I wanted to mention that Mrs. Maitland has been very impressed with your work," Miss Cohen went on.

"Oh, that's great." Dan grinned. Paul clapped his brother on the shoulder.

"And she's a significant figure in our little community of art lovers," Miss Cohen said, a smile tugging at her lips. "A patron with both a discerning eye and the desire to support emerging talent such as yourself. As well as having the means to do so."

"Really?" Dan's ears perked up. He glanced at Paul. His brother grinned back.

"Indeed." She stopped for a second to wave goodnight to another student before returning her attention to Dan. She continued. "She knows artistic potential when she sees it. As well as what she likes."

"Potential, huh?" Paul chimed in, unable to contain his curiosity. "Does that mean what I think it does?"

"Mrs. Maitland's been quite taken with your portfolio, what she's seen displayed in the hallway exhibits," the art instructor said, not directly answering Paul. "She wishes to commission you for a project of hers."

"Me? A commission?" Dan reiterated, his pulse quickening at the idea. "Wow... that's... that's neat. What kind is it?"

"Portraits," Miss Cohen answered. "Of Max and Brutus."

"Are those her children?" Dan asked, the image of two freckle-faced troublemakers already forming in his mind's eye.

"Her dogs," Miss Cohen said, her tone flat as if it were the most natural thing in the world.

Paul spat out a chortle, which he tried to disguise as a cough. It didn't work; his eyes gave him away.

"Dogs," Dan confirmed.

"Indeed," Miss Cohen said dryly, "And she's willing to pay handsomely for their likenesses. A hundred dollars, to be precise."

"Wait, what? A C-Note? To paint a pair of pooches' portraits?" Paul's smile faltered as the number settled in.

Dan turned to his brother. "Excellent. A quadruple alliteration."

Paul inclined his head in appreciation. "Thank you."

"A hundred dollars," Miss Cohen said again, nodding solemnly. "For a painting incorporating the two dogs. I must warn you, Dan. She has definite ideas as to what she wants. And she can be quite demanding."

"Hey, for a hundred bucks, I'll paint whatever she says. And that includes her garage!" Dan said. "The money would pay most of my tuition next year at City College!"

"Guess it's time to unleash your inner Da Vinci, my dear brother," Paul said, the initial shock giving way to a grin. "Who knew Fido and Rover were worth their weight in cash?"

"Brutus and Max," Dan corrected automatically. He took a deep breath and stood tall, matching his brother's height. "I'm ready for the challenges of capturing canine charisma on canvas."

He held up five fingers to Paul. His twin politely applauded with the fingertips of one hand into the open palm of the other, nodding in approval.

Miss Cohen's puzzled gaze moved between the siblings. "Are you two like this all the time?"

"No. Usually, I dominate him effortlessly," Paul returned.

"I allow him to have his little fantasies," Dan said.

Miss Cohen looked confused for a second, then laughed. She handed Dan a small card. "Here is her phone number. She'll be expecting your call."

Dan took it and stared at the sliver of cardboard as it was made of solid gold. "Thank you, Miss Cohen."

"Let me know what happens next week. Good luck, Dan," Miss Cohen said.

"I will! Thank you! Good night!" Dan waved.

The art instructor headed for the door. She called over her shoulder, "Last person to leave, please turn off the lights."

Dan placed the phone number in his wallet with care, then continued to put away his supplies.

"David here is going to change now," Paul said. "His marbles are getting cold." He shuffled off to the makeshift changing area.

"Hey, Dan," the grumpy man from class approached and leaned in like a conspirator. He was the sort of person who always seemed to carry a cloud of suspicion about everything. Things like he was positive Adolf Hitler escaped Germany at the end of the war and was living on a South American banana plantation.

"Uh, yeah?" Dan said, raising an eyebrow.

"Before you go painting dogs in mansions, I think you oughta let you in on something," Mr. Jenkins spoke in a quiet voice, glancing around as if invisible spies might bet lurking among the easels.

"Okay...?" Dan replied, a little baffled at what his classmate was getting at.

"That place of Mrs. Maitland's — that mansion — it's haunted." The old man cocked one bushy eyebrow and dropped to a dramatic hush. "Spirits, specters, ghouls — the whole shebang."

"Ha... haunted?" Dan swallowed. A small part of him never could shake the feeling that something supernatural lurked in the darkness every time he heard a strange noise. Of course, his rational mind refused to believe in such things. He just wasn't anxious to find out if his rational mind was wrong.

"When something goes bump in the night in that place, it ain't the plumbing." Mr. Jenkins jammed his index finger at Dan to emphasize his point. "Don't say old Jenkins didn't warn ya. That joint has a history darker than a black cat in a coal mine at midnight."

"Thank you for the warning," Dan said. He tried for some humor to take the edge off his nerves. It was a swing and a miss. "I'll wear a garlic necklace and bring oil for the spirits' chains."

"Make light of it now, son," the older artist continued, unfazed, "But mark my words, those halls echo more than just the pitter-patter of a couple of pampered dogs."

"I'm sorry, sir, I know you mean well, but I don't believe in ghosts," Dan said with what he intended to be firmness. He glanced around nervously, as though one was lurking in the corner. "But I always speak well of them."

"All right, kid. Just thought you ought to know." The old man grumbled as he shuffled out, his warning hanging in the air like the chalk dust that never quite settled in the old classroom.

A spooky voice wailed in the room. "What evil stalks the halls of Maitland Manor at midnight? It is I, the phantom! OOOOOHHHHHH!"

A figure draped in the curtain of the changing booth walked toward Dan. It waved its arms and moaned. Dan stepped up and kicked the specter in the shins. The spirit yelled "ow!". Dan pulled the material off his brother.

"That's the way I do ghostbusting." Dan jerked his thumb toward himself.

Paul stopped rubbing his shin. "And a very effective way, too."

"Now put that back where it belongs, and let's get home. I'm sure you want to slip into your nice, warm casket." Dan slung the satchel over his shoulder and grinned. "Turn out the lights, Boris."

Chapter Two

With a deep breath, Dan tried to calm his nerves as he crossed to the small desk in the Case family living room. He exhaled before picking up the receiver and dialing the number on the card Miss Cohen had given him. He readied a pen and poised it over a yellow notepad, preparing to note any important information Mrs. Maitland might share. As he waited for someone to pick up at the other end of the line, Dan cleared his throat and began counting the rings.

"Hello?" The answering voice was smooth and rich, like hot fudge pouring over ice cream.

"Uh, hi, Mrs. Maitland, this is Dan Case," he stammered, trying not to sound as tongue-tied as the first time he asked his girlfriend Donna out for a date.

"Ah, Daniel." Her tone wrapped around his name like a velvet glove. "I'm delighted you called. I've viewed your work at the Adult Education Center, and I'm most impressed."

"Thank you." Dan actually gave a little bow, as though Mrs. Maitland could see it on the other end of the line.

"As Miss Cohen must have informed you, I'd wish to commission you to paint a portrait of Brutus and Max."

"Yes. She told me." Dan hoped he sounded calm and professional... like this was nothing out of the ordinary. But he doubted it.

"I've been imagining this English-style painting, with Brutus and Max, posed in front of the mansion. The masters of the estate," Mrs. Mailtand went on. "A pastoral idyll, if you will."

"Sounds like something I can do," Dan said. "I could come out, take some photos for reference, then go to work in my... uh, studio."

That was a made-up, grand term for the old workshop built along the garage he and his brother shared. Dan's easel, sketchbook, and art supplies took up one half, while Paul's boxing equipment and speed bag took up the other.

"Oh, no. Photographs won't do, I'm afraid. I wish the work painted plein aire, Daniel," Mrs. Maitland said.

She used the correct French pronunciation of the term — meaning 'painting outside' — with some pride, Dan thought.

"There's a certain *je ne sais quoi* about capturing the light and essence of a locale at the moment, don't you agree?" Mrs. Maitland asked.

"Oh, yes. That's the way I paint most of my landscapes. Plein aire would let me capture the spirit of the mansion," Dan said. He scribbled 'plein aire' on the pad, underlining it twice. "So, maybe I can scout the, uh, locale first? It will help me with the composition before I do the actual painting."

"But of course! That is essential," she said. "And while you're there, why not bring your brushes? The grounds are simply divine this time of year."

"Divine" wasn't a word Dan heard often. The last time was when he was at work behind the soda fountain. That's what a customer called the triple chocolate sundae he made. "Sure. My sketchbook goes with me wherever I go. I'll also take my camera since I doubt Max and Brutus would pose for me..."

Mrs. Maitland giggled. "No, they wouldn't! They are such devilish little scamps!"

Dan pictured a pair of small yapping dust mops on legs. "So I'll take some photos of them, and I can get a sense of the place."

"Marvelous! Then can you come out Friday after school?"

"Well... I don't know. I can switch my work schedule at the soda fountain, but my brother and I share a jeep. He does landscaping, and he needs it during the weekends. That's true now since it's spring. He's very busy. And it's quite a drive to your estate." Dan saw his commission evaporating before his eyes. He thought out loud. "Mom could—"

"Is that all? A question of transportation?" Mrs. Maitland chuckled. "Dear boy, please don't fret about such trifles. I will send Romero to fetch you."

"Romero?"

"Ricardo Romero, our chauffeur," she clarified. "He will ensure you arrive in safety and comfort to begin your artistic odyssey. You may remain overnight as my guest as well. Romero will deliver you to your home the next day. Does that alleviate your concerns, Daniel?"

"Sure," Dan said. "That sounds… great."

"Wonderful," Mrs. Maitland purred. "Oh, and we don't dress for dinner."

For one anxious second, Dan thought the Maitlands were nudists until he realized she meant they didn't "dress up" for dinner. That relaxed him somewhat, but he decided he would still wear his best pair of jeans, newest sneakers, and a button-down shirt, anyway.

"Romero will collect you Friday afternoon," Mrs. Maitland said. "I eagerly anticipate your arrival."

"Friday it is," Dan said, although 'collect' made him feel like a rare postage stamp. "I'll see you then. Goodbye." He set the receiver down with a soft click.

His first commission. He glanced at a framed photograph of a smiling young man in an army uniform resting on the mantle. Next to the photo hung a small, rectangular banner with a blue border and gold star. Dan's father would have been proud. He punched his fist in the air in celebration.

***

Friday afternoon, Paul threw open the door and stepped into the workshop, holding Dan's overnight bag. "His Majesty's carriage awaits!" he intoned in a terrible British accent.

"Oh, shut up." Dan slipped his sketchbook and some pencils into his satchel. He reached for his camera bag.

"Allow me, sire." Paul swept up the bag with a flourish worthy of the finest footman in Buckingham Palace. He continued, adopting the stiff posture of the elite staff they'd seen in movies. "Shall I announce dinner next, or would you prefer me to draw your tepid bathwater first?"

Dan jabbed his finger at his twin. "You know, I think I'm going to exile you to Australia."

Paul arched an eyebrow behind his glasses. "What, again, sir?"

"Permanently, this time." Dan waved his brother off. "You can box the kangaroos. They'd win, though."

They made their way out of the workshop. Mrs. Case stood on the back porch. She was an attractive woman in her mid-thirties, equipped with an unexpected toughness that served her when she had to go toe-to-toe with city council members or meter readers as the first woman county water department manager. She performed a formal curtsy to Dan.

"Best of luck, Sir Daniel," she called as she waved. "May your quest be filled with grandeur and... minimal dog drool."

"Thanks, Mom." Dan rolled his eyes but grinned at her playful send-off. He muttered to himself. "This family is full of comedians."

The twins walked down the driveway to the front of their house. A massive vehicle — a deep green Cadillac Fleetwood — stood next to the curb, its shiny exterior reflecting the sunlight. Standing by the open trunk was Ricardo Romero, the Maitland's chauffeur.

Despite his shorter stature compared to Dan, his muscular frame packed out his black and gray uniform with ease. His chiseled features and movie-star good looks would have caused Donna to swoon then and there.

Romero took the luggage from Paul and placed it in the trunk, closing the lid. Dan started toward the car's front passenger door.

"Mr. Case," Romero instructed. His voice, highlighted by a slight Spanish accent, was smooth and unruffled as the limousine's comfortable seats. He opened the rear door.

Dan blushed a moment in a mix of embarrassment and discomfort. He couldn't believe he missed he was supposed to ride in the back. Now he felt awkward as he climbed into it like he didn't belong in it at all. He settled into the soft embrace of the upholstery, the interior smelling of leather.

As the chauffeur closed the door and moved to the driver's seat, Dan looked out the tinted glass. Mrs. Case and Paul stood next to each other on the lawn, grinning. They waved. Dan returned one of his own and leaned back. The limousine's engine started, a rumble that suggested power and politeness at the same time.

The Cadillac approached the only traffic light in Dan's hometown of Farmingford, slowed, and whispered to a quiet stop. Dan turned his head towards the passenger window and smiled when he saw Ted, a fellow soda jerk at Allen's Drugstore, sitting on his bike next to the car.

They had traded shifts for the day, and Ted was dressed for work: black shoes, black pants, and a long-sleeved white shirt, with the collar unbuttoned and the silly clip-on bowtie hanging from one side. When Ted noticed Dan inside the luxurious car, his jaw dropped in surprise. Dan grinned, gave a nod of acknowledgment, and saluted as the Cadillac drove away.

The limousine glided past the storefronts of the small village — the post office with its iconic mailbox, the daycare center vibrant with children's artwork, and the library branch. The church was just as picturesque, with a pristine white steeple rising into the pale blue sky, guarded by a majestic oak tree. Farther down the road stood the town hall, a grand brick building adorned with towering pillars and a clock that ticked away each passing second.

Leaving town, the highway meandered through the hills and woods that stretched from Farmingford to Belmont. The dense forest of oaks and maples crowded the pavement. Scattered among the trees were many small family farms, passed down through generations since the 1800s. Somehow, these familiar sights appeared different when viewed from the back seat of a chauffeured Cadillac Fleetwood.

With nothing but the hum of the road for company, Dan figured he might as well try to strike up a conversation with Romero. "So, how long have you been driving for the Maitlands?" he asked, leaning forward.

"For only two months," came the succinct reply. For a moment, Romero's black eyes — a piercing, intense gaze that could slice through glass — met Dan's in the rearview mirror before returning to look out the windshield.

"Do you like driving?" Dan tried to keep the conversation going.

"More than some jobs," Romero answered.

A mile or so passed.

"Have you done this type of work before?" Dan tried again.

"I drove a general around during the war."

"Oh. Where did you serve?"

"Italy."

Silence fell. So much for small talk. It was clear to Dan that Romero had closed the book on their chat. Maybe there's a rule in chauffeurs' contracts about not talking with the passengers in the rear. Dan settled back in his seat. He gazed out the window at the passing scenery.

The limousine glided past Belmont, hugging the highway that snaked along the steep banks of the broad Kobalt River. Several boats dotted the water's deep blue surface, from simple rowboats to even a few grand cabin cruisers. The car crossed a soaring iron trestle bridge and turned onto a two-lane road on the other side. Through the breaks in the lush green trees, sprawling estates peeked out, almost shyly, as if trying to hide their grandeur. The Cadillac entered a gravel drive that split through a row of yew trees. They drove past a small cottage and rumbled forward.

Dan's eyes widened as he caught sight of what lay ahead. The Maitland Mansion loomed over the landscape, a formidable testament to the long ago extravagance of the late nineteenth-century Gilded Age. The house seemed to have sprung straight out of a vivid medieval tapestry. Built of stone, the manor resembled a smaller version of a European castle, transplanted and put in this very spot. Turrets and towers punctuated its tall, stately walls. The only thing missing was a moat, though the nearby river served as a suitable substitute.

"Never thought I'd be stepping into a fairy tale," Dan said under his breath. He half-expected knights in armor to be lounging around outside, playing ping-pong or doing whatever lounging knights did in their free time.

Romero barely graced him with a glance. The Cadillac's tires crunched the driveway's gravel as they approached the front entrance, flanked by lawns so green they looked airbrushed, and beds of vibrant daffodils greeting the spring. The limo stopped under a portico next to a pair of carved wooden doors, the chauffeur sliding out of the driver's seat. He already had the back door open, while Dan was fumbling to find the handle.

"This way please, sir," Romero intoned. Following the chauffeur up four granite steps, Dan stepped into the mansion.

"Please wait here, Mr. Case," Romero said. "I'll get Mrs. Maitland."

Dan looked around the foyer. It matched the exterior. Smooth flagstone, cool and polished under his feet, made up the floors. Ornate wood paneling adorned every wall, designs etched into the rich oak. The few pieces of furniture were dark and heavy, each piece decorated with intricate, carved fine details. A suit of armor stood in one corner as though on guard, holding a battleaxe aloft, its metal gleaming in the soft light. An imposing staircase, steps covered in a ruby red carpet, angled up to the floors above. Romero returned.

"Mrs. Maitland will be here. I will take your luggage to your room," the chauffeur said.

"Thank you."

Mrs. Maitland entered the foyer, every inch of her displaying grace and refinement. Despite her middle years, her silver hair shimmered like strands of moonlight. She was dressed in a simple but attractive blue dress, well-tailored to stress her slender figure. Around her neck, a strand of lustrous pearls added an air of sophistication.

"And you must be Daniel!" Mrs. Mailand trilled. She extended her hand. "I'm so pleased to meet you. I'm an admirer of your art."

Dan gave her hand a brief shake. "Thank you. I appreciate that. I'm pleased to meet you. This place is... incredible."

"It is indeed," Mrs. Maitland said. Romero came back into the foyer, Dan's suitcase, satchel, and camera bag in hand. He mounted the stairs to the second floor. "Now, Daniel, I must introduce you to your subjects at once! The little darlings should be around here somewhere! I always lose track of them. Max! Brutus! Come, boys!"

The clicking of sharp claws against the cool stone floor announced two massive Great Danes, one black and one tan. They paused for a moment, their heads cocked in curiosity, then galloped towards Dan with reckless abandon. Before he could even react, they bowled Dan off his feet and smothered him with playful paws and eager wet noses. He let out a muffled "Oh boy—" as he struggled beneath their weight.

"Brutus! Max! Gentle! Gentle! Remember, play nice!" Mrs. Maitland scolded half-heartedly as she wagged a finger at the dogs. She laughed. "Oh, they get so excited when they meet new people! Aren't they the cutest little things?"

Max — or Brutus, Dan didn't know which was which — slurped a tongue up his cheek. "Yeah..."

"Alright, boys, that's enough playtime." Mrs. Maitland clapped her hands twice and gave a sharp command. "Sit!"

To Dan's surprise, Max and Brutus obeyed in an instant.

"Guess I'm part of the pack now," Dan said, as he struggled to his feet. He brushed off dog slobber from his jacket while the dogs waited, their large heads tilting in tandem as they regarded their new playmate.

"Oh, Brutus is the black one, and Max is the tan one. It seems they've taken quite a liking to you," Mrs. Maitland said. She leaned toward Dan and spoke in a low voice, as though letting him in on a secret. "Scratch them behind the ears. Go on."

Using both hands, one per animal, Dan scratched Brutus and Max in the indicated spot. The Great Danes' tails thumped against the floor.

"Now that you are acquainted, I'll bring Andrew. Excuse me for a moment." Mrs. Maitland bustled out.

Dan chuckled while stroking Brutus and Max, but he glimpsed movement from the corner of his eye. He shifted his gaze to see Romero standing like a statue on the staircase. Dan couldn't help but wonder how much of the scene Romero had seen, but the chauffeur's face remained impassive as he quietly exited through the front entrance.

"Andrew, come meet our artist!" Mrs. Maitland's voice echoed down the hall. She stepped into the foyer, followed a few seconds later by a young man, perhaps 23 or 24 years old, sauntering behind her. "Daniel, this is my son, Andrew."

He was slender and stood an inch or two taller than Dan. His wavy brown hair was artfully styled, perfectly framing his angular face and fashionable glasses. Dressed in crisp white from head to toe, he looked like he was either on his way to or from the tennis court. His outfit, accented with a sweater draped over his shoulders, gave off an air of carefully curated casualness. His contrasting tan broadcast spending the winter where the sun always shined. Andrew's expression seemed to be parked somewhere between haughty and forever bored.

It was clear to Dan that nobody never, ever, called Mrs. Maitland's son "Andy".

"Pleased to meet you," Andrew drawled, although not one facial muscle budged.

"Likewise," Dan replied.

"And now let us dine." Mrs. Maitland led Dan and Andrew into the dining room, where a long table with twelve chairs awaited them.

Wooden beams ran across the ceiling, adding to the rustic charm of the room. Mounted heads of elk, deer, and a fierce boar adorned the walls, giving the space the feeling of a baronial hall from medieval Europe. Gleaming place settings lay on the tabletop in front of three seats. A matronly woman dressed in a navy blue dress and frilly apron — and an expression as sour as unsweetened lemonade — stood by a carved oak sideboard loaded with serving dishes.

"You may serve, Mrs. Danner." Mrs. Maitland sat at the head of the table. A salad was placed before her. "So, Daniel, what is your perspective on the employment of color in Van Gogh's later works?"

The array of silverware overwhelmed Dan arranged around the place setting, probably more than his family even owned, trying to remember which piece to use first. He was thankful for a conversational topic he could talk about. "The vibrancy—it's like he was struggling to capture the intensity of his feelings on the canvas," he answered. He noted which fork Mrs. Maitland used and did the same.

Across from Dan, Andrew poked at his food, his bored expression unchanging. The young man's silence hung in the air, a contrast to the animated discussion between his mother and their guest.

Dinner concluded, with Mrs. Danner clearing away the plates. Her movement was so silent and efficient, it was as though the dishes disappeared of their own accord. Mrs. Maitland rose and beckoned them to follow her to the living room, a grand space with high ceilings and French doors leading to the terrace. Two plush velvet sofas sat facing each other. A pair of elegant wing chairs flanked an impressive fireplace. The real eye-catcher, however, was a polished mahogany cabinet holding a television set.

The Case family didn't own a TV yet, so Dan had only seen them before in store windows. Sitting on one sofa, he watched with wide-eyed curiosity as the ten-inch screen buzzed to life.

"Television is such a fascinating invention, don't you think, Daniel?" Mrs. Maitland fiddled with the knobs. She gave a few polite taps to the side of the set. "That helps the picture. Television is a portal to worlds beyond our own, all from the comfort of our armchairs. Culture beamed directly into our own living rooms."

She turned to face Dan and Andrew, speaking as though announcing the next selection from a symphony program. "Tonight, we have a special treat. 'Wrestling from Marigold', broadcast out of Chicago. Gorgeous George versus Ed 'Strangler' Lewis."

Rolling his eyes, Andrew took the other sofa, while Mrs. Maitland sat in another wing chair placed near the set. Max and Brutus trotted in and flopped down by Dan's seat.

The glowing black-and-white image on the screen revealed burly men in tight leotards grappling with each other on a square mat. When one wrestler took a particularly dramatic fall, Mrs. Maitland jumped to her feet, shouting advice and admonishments with the vigor of a seasoned coach. His host's transformation startled Dan.

"Come on, Strangler! Do you call that a body slam? My grandmother could take you down with her eyes closed!" Mrs. Maitland bellowed.

Andrew, however, remained impassive, lounging with one ankle resting on his knee. His only reaction was an occasional arched brow or a slight shake of his head as if he were watching an uninspired chess match.

Dan was so entranced by the TV that he didn't realize it had begun to rain until Mrs. Maitland finally stood and switched the set off. She pushed back some loose strands of hair.

"That's enough television for tonight, I think. We mustn't get addicted to it!" she warned with a smile, then listened for a moment. "Oh, it seems to have started raining. The spring weather is so fickle. Well, Daniel, breakfast is laid out at 8:00 am. It's a buffet. Come down when you're ready. Your room is the first door on the left at the top of the stairs. Good night."

Both Dan and Andrew stood, adding their good nights, as Mrs. Maitland left. With a final, inscrutable look at Dan, Andrew soon trailed after his mother. Dan glanced at the silent black television screen, vowing to use some of his commission to buy one for his family. He padded upstairs.

His room was filled with rich, dark wood paneling that gave warmth and elegance to the space. Against one wall was a four-poster bed, imposing and regal, its rich, carved headboard reaching towards the ceiling. Across sat a massive dresser and mirror, its intricate details catching the light. Plush velvet drapes framed the tall windows.

He got ready for bed, marveling at how wonderful it was to have his own bathroom, and not compete with his mother and brother for their home's only one. Finishing brushing his teeth, he climbed between the soft covers and turned off the lamp.

A deafening clap of thunder shook the house, sending the sound reverberating through the corridors like a stampede of bowling balls. The door to the room rattled as something crashed against it from the other side. Dan got up and cracked the door.

Max and Brutus wedged their way inside the room before he had the door completely open. They looked up at him with big, pleading eyes, shivering, with their tails tucked between their legs.

"Okay, okay, guys, you can stay with me. There's room in the bed," Dan said with a laugh. He lifted the covers to allow the quaking canines sanctuary under the bedspread.

He went back to the door. Just as he was about to shut it, a sudden burst of brilliant lightning lit up the hall in a stark, white flare. At that moment, Dan spotted a tall figure standing at the far end of the corridor, silhouetted in the window. The thing appeared to be draped in a dark, hooded cloak, like a monk's habit.

As quickly as the light had come, darkness swallowed the scene whole. But another flash of lightning showed the person — or whatever it was — had disappeared without a trace. Mr. Jenkin's warnings about the Maitland house flooded into Dan's mind. He shivered.

Dan closed the door. And locked it. Not that it would do any good against ghosts.

"Move over, fellas," Dan said to the dogs. "I'm joining you under the covers."

Chapter Three

Dan entered the dining room the next morning. Mrs. Maitland again sat at the head of the table, finishing her breakfast. Andrew, hidden behind the newspaper, occupied the same seat as dinner.

"Good morning, Daniel," Mrs. Maitland greeted with a smile. Andrew dropped his paper briefly and nodded. "Did the storm keep you awake last night?"

"No, it didn't." That was true, although Dan wondering if that strange hallway apparition would decide to pop into his room for a visit did.

"I'm glad to hear it. It was a doozy, wasn't it?" She waved to the sideboard. "There are eggs, toast, bacon, potatoes, and coffee. Please help yourself."

"Thank you." Dan loaded his plate with food and sat down.

"What are your plans today, Daniel?" Mrs. Maitland delicately picked up a slice of toast, keeping her pinky finger raised as she took a dainty bite.

"I plan to make some sketches and take some photographs of Max and Brutus. For reference," Dan said as he began his breakfast.

"Here's something interesting," Andrew said from in back of his paper. "The police have some new leads in the Black Dahlia murder case." He lowered the newspaper and spoke to Dan with about as much emotion as discussing railroad timetables. "You know the case? Last year in Los Angeles, Elizabeth Short's body was found. It was severed in half at the waist and completely drained of blood—"

Mrs. Maitland's voice dropped an octave. "Andrew, please, not while we're eating."

Andrew shrugged and went back to the news. The ketchup Dan put on his scrambled eggs now made them unappetizing.

"When do you plan to start the actual painting?" Mrs. Maitland went on.

"Well, I was thinking since school spring vacation starts next week—" Dan began.

Mrs. Maitland clasped her hands together. "Perfect! Romero will collect you after school on Friday, then you can stay here while you apply brush to canvas! Is that acceptable to you?"

Dan grinned. "Sure. That sounds great."

"Excellent. I'm afraid I can't remain here today. The Women's Club is holding our annual Spring Fête, although some people insist on calling it by the common term of a 'rummage sale'." She shook her head in disbelief. "I am in charge of the pricing committee, so I will be spending all day at the clubhouse marking our treasures! You know how that is!"

Dan didn't but pretended he did.

"So I'll leave you in the capable hands of Andrew. He'll show you around the estate. Afterward, you can make yourself at home.

Let the atmosphere soak into you. Inspire you," Mrs. Maitland said with a flair.

"That will be fine," Dan said.

"Well, I'm off. Romero will return to take you to your house at approximately 3:00, Daniel." Mrs. Maitland stood and gave her son a peck on his cheek as she passed behind his chair. She continued speaking to her son in an "and I mean it" tone. "Be friendly to our guest now."

Andrew sighed a weary "Of course, Mother."

"Until next week, Daniel." Mrs. Maitland waved and hurried out of the room.

Dan finished his breakfast in silence as Andrew continued to read his paper. When Dan was done, Andrew folded up his newspaper and got up.

"Right this way, Daniel. I'll show you around." Andrew gestured with the disinterested air of a tour guide who had walked these halls a thousand times.

"I prefer Dan."

"Fine." It was clear Andrew didn't care one way or the other what Dan preferred.

Max and Brutus waited outside the dining room. They followed as Dan and Andrew strolled down the main hall. Its walls were adorned with carved panels and heavy beams crisscrossing the ceiling. Along the sides of the hallway hung several portraits, their subjects staring out at the viewers with a kind of disappointed judgment.

"Your ancestors?" Dan asked, gesturing at the artwork.

Andrew shook his head. "I have no idea who they are. The house was purchased with all its contents. Everything you see."

"So you only had to bring your toothbrush?" Dan grinned. Andrew cracked a polite smile in response. "So they're antiques?"

Andrew shrugged. "Sure. It's just old furniture to me. Same thing with the decor, like these paintings. We've added only one painting here." He paused before a grand portrait of a man, perhaps in his forties. The figure painted was dignified and regal, seated behind a desk full of important-looking papers. "This is my father. Amos Maitland."

"I can see the resemblance," Dan said. He examined the painting a little closer. "It's well executed."

"Should be. It cost enough."

"Well, I look forward to meeting Mr. Maitland in real life one day. Find out how true the likeness is," Dan said.

"Father 'isn't here,'" Andrew said cryptically.

Dan jumped to a conclusion. He assumed the senior Maitland shared more than just perhaps a military background with his own late father. "I'm sorry. My... my dad was killed in action. On D-Day."

"I'm sorry to hear that," Andrew said. "But no, my father isn't dead. He's simply... abroad. Hasn't lived in the country for years now. He... left just before the war."

"Ah." Dan's cheeks reddened at the misunderstanding.

Andrew broke the awkward quiet. He swung open a pair of double doors. "This is the library."

Floor-to-ceiling bookcases lined the walls, overflowing with books. Andrew made a dry comment that the previous owner must have "bought books by the yard". The scent of old paper and leather filled the room. Next came a small, bright morning room illuminated by large windows. Mrs. Maitland's petite desk sat in the middle of the space. A blotter, bordered in a flowery pattern, lay on the top. A matching pen holder, perpetual calendar, and paperclip holder occupied precise positions. A glass paperweight — crystal, Dan assumed from the way it sparkled in the light — rested in the middle of the blotter. Dan and Andrew returned to the hall.

"I've saved the best for last. Let me show you the most interesting room in the house. It's usually locked. Mother despises it, but it's my favorite," he said as they neared a wooden door, reaching for the iron key hanging near it. He inserted the key and turned it until the door unlocked with a loud clunk. Pushing it open, the heavy hinges groaned in protest under the weight of the door.

Dan peered past Andrew at the top of a dark set of steps leading to the basement. "What's down there?"

Andrew glanced at Dan and responded without a trace of a smile. "It's the torture chamber."

"A what?" Dan asked, wondering if he had heard Andrew correctly.

"A torture chamber," Andrew said again. "I'm sure you've noticed this house was designed to resemble a castle. Apparently, when the old coot — one Joshua Collins — built the place, he thought every well-fitted castle needed a dungeon, so he added one. Come on."

Andrew flipped a light switch. Sconces resembling torches with flame-shaped bulbs lined the stone walls of the stairway. He started down. Dan hesitated a second, then went after his host. After a few steps, he glanced behind him. Brutus and Max remained in the doorway.

"The dogs..." Dan pointed.

"Oh, they never come down here." Andrew continued downstairs without looking back or breaking stride.

"Shows they're not so stupid," Dan said under his breath as he followed down. He half-expected the ghostly monk from last night to float past, going the other way.

At the bottom of the stairs, Dan ended up alone in a small room, with doors on three walls. "Andrew?"

Andrew's voice came from behind the door on the right. "In here."

With a grunt, Dan heaved open the thick wooden door and stepped into a dark dungeon. The oppressive atmosphere of the room weighed down on him at once, as if the very air was heavy with doom. The dim light from electric torches mounted on the walls provided little relief, only serving to cast ominous shadows across the space.

On two walls, manacles dangled menacingly. An open iron maiden stood tall and foreboding on the opposite wall, its sharp spikes protruding. A brassiere, holding metal rods ready to be heated to red-hot, loomed in one corner and a gibbet stood in another. Axes and hatchets were arrayed along the walls, their edges gleaming with malice. Cat-o'-nine-tails and coiled whips hung next to them. But it was the rack dominating the center of the room that sent a true chill down Dan's spine, completing the grim decor.

The door behind him slammed closed. Dan gasped and spun around.

"Who knows what ghastly happenings occurred in rooms such as this?" Andrew's voice echoed in the dreary place.

Dan turned back to look in the room. He couldn't find the source of the sound.

"How many people screamed their lives away in dank dungeons like these, writhing in untold agony, their pleas for mercy falling on uncaring ears?" Andrew intoned.

"Yeah." Dan's voice cracked. He swallowed.

Andrew emerged from the darkness of one corner, the shadows peeling away like cobwebs. He slowly walked toward Dan, a long knife held in one hand. "Imagine how horrible it was to face a bleak future of unending, excruciating pain!" He stopped and raised the knife with a dramatic flair.

Grasping the blade with his other hand, he bent the weapon back and forth, then tossed it casually on the rack. He went on in a casual tone. "It's rubber. The door was built out of plumb on purpose, so it closes by itself."

"Oh... yeah," Dan chuckled. It was unconvincing. "So everything down here is fake?"

"Well, most of it is. I think the rack is an original from some castle or other in Europe. The axes and the spikes in the iron maiden are also rubber. Harmless stage props. This room gave my parents the idea of hosting Halloween parties." He smiled at the memory. "They were *the* social event of the fall season. We decorated the whole mansion. Down here, we had onion dip and chips on the rack, and cheese fondue heated on the brassiere. We even provided costumes for everyone to wear. There's a room full of them next door. My father liked to dress me up as the executioner and posted me in here. It was grand fun."

"I'll bet. Talk about a rumpus room," Dan said, picturing Mr. Maitland reveling among guests dressed as ghouls and phantoms. It was hard not to imagine the clanking of chains echoing off the walls, mingled with laughter and eerie music. All accompanied by tasty hors d'oeuvres.

The two returned to the hall, where the light felt both warmer and safer to Dan. As much as he enjoyed reading mysteries, he avoided ghost stories. That creepy dungeon reminded him of why. While he scratched Brutus and Max behind their ears, Andrew locked the heavy door.

Dan recalled the mysterious figure he had seen the previous night. "Is there anything else unusual about this house?"

"I always considered having a dungeon to be rather unusual."

"Well, yes, but what about... you know, supernatural stuff?" Dan asked. "The way the house is designed, and as old as it is, I could see something moving in."

"What, ghosts? Spooks?" Andrew waved one hand in disdain. "If you mean that, no. I've never heard of one."

They crossed the hall and entered the living room, stepping out onto the terrace. The green lawn sloped down from the house.

"This is the rest of the estate. We sold the northern half of the property when Father... we sold it. Our land now extends down to the canal," Andrew said.

"A canal?" Dan asked.

Andrew nodded. "Before the railroad arrived, this part of the country had several canals built in the late 1800s to transport goods. One runs between the river and Benson Lake. There used to be a mill up there. The state maintains it now as a recreational waterway. Over there is the tennis court. Do you play?"

Dan shook his head.

"Pity." Andrew gestured to the other places of interest. "To the left is the hedge maze. When Collins discovered that Hampton Court Palace in England had one, he wanted one, too. Oh, and that small stone building is his crypt. Don't worry, it's not occupied. When he died, he was buried in Toledo. And that ends your nickel tour. I suppose you wish to start with your artistic activities now."

"Yes. I'll get my sketchbook and camera, then I'll scout around outside for a view of the house that will work for the painting," Dan said.

"Fine. Oh, you may run into the gardener out there. His name is Albert Lang... if he deigns to speak to you at all. And if you require any refreshment, see Mrs. Danner in the kitchen. I'll be somewhere about if you have questions." Andrew strolled back into the house without waiting to find out if there were any.

Dan went back to his room, Max and Brutus in tow. He pulled his sketchbook out of his luggage and slung the camera around his neck. He spoke to the dogs. "Well, guys, let's hunt up the perfect place for your portrait."

Coming down the staircase, Dan caught sight of Andrew in the foyer with his back to him, collecting the mail from a table near the front door. Dan paused for a moment, although he honestly didn't know why. Even Brutus and Max halted.

Andrew sorted through the envelopes until he stopped at one. His body went rigid as he stared at the letter in his hand. After a few quick glances to his left and right to ensure no one was watching, he hastily folded the envelope in half and tucked it into his back pocket. He tossed the rest of the mail back on the table before making a hasty exit from the foyer.

"Odd," Dan said to himself. He shrugged. It wasn't his concern. Perhaps it was a note from an ex-flame of Andrew's. Or an overdue bill.

With Max and Brutus bounding ahead of him, Dan stepped onto the sprawling grounds of the estate. The mature trees stretched their branches overhead, casting a dappled shade over the flower beds that dotted the landscape. As he passed one bed, he saw the haphazard arrangement of flowers and weeds.

Paul would love to get hold of that plot of ground, Dan thought. A few of his brother's customers were so impressed with his knack with plants that they asked him to design their gardens, a task he greatly enjoyed. Dan helped by drawing the plans.

Maybe he could drop Paul's name to Mrs. Maitland... Then he remembered Andrew mentioning a gardener who tended to the property. Dan guessed that this particular garden had yet to receive his attention.

Dan strolled down the long, winding driveway until he was almost at the road. He turned around and studied the mansion before him. Searching for the perfect background for his painting, he paced to his left, keeping his gaze fixed on the house. He checked how the angles changed, how the light danced over different parts of the house, and how the perspective shifted, as he looked for that one correct vantage point. The perfect spot was by the tennis court.

The house sat on higher ground than the court. Dan glanced back and forth between the imposing structure and the dogs, imagining where they would fit in his composition. A smile formed on his face — this would be the ideal location.

He attempted to capture a photo of both Brutus and Max together, but they always wanted to play with him and wouldn't stay still at the same time. Even his tries at imitating Mrs. Maitland's "sit" command failed. Eventually, he could snap some shots of each one separately in a semi-posed position, giving him some material to work with for the painting.

Settling onto a bench next to the court, Dan opened his sketchbook and began drawing. His small, rough sketches helped him plan the painting's composition, where to place the dogs, and how much of the house to show.

As usual, he lost himself in his craft, consumed by his art. It was quiet except for the sound of the birds and the rustling of leaves. A shadow slid across the page. Dan stood and spun around. Romero stood behind him, a silent sentinel, watching him work.

"I'm sorry if I startled you, Mr. Case," the chauffeur said. "I didn't wish to interrupt you. You seemed so engrossed in your task."

"That's all right." Dan closed his sketchbook and got up. He said to himself, "Maybe you should wear a bell around your neck."

"Mrs. Maitland wishes me to drive you back to your home," Romero said. "Are you ready, sir?"

"Yes. Just let me get my things." Dan shouldered his camera.

"The car is waiting for you out front, Mr. Case."

Dan walked back to the house. As he did, he saw Andrew exiting through the French doors onto the terrace. Dan waved, but Andrew didn't acknowledge him. The younger Maitland headed towards a group of hedges, Dan assuming it was the maze. Without looking around, Andrew walked swiftly and disappeared into the maze.

Dan quickly packed his bag in his room and went outside to find Brutus and Max standing by the car, their tails wagging.

"See you guys next week." Dan scratched the dogs behind their ears as Romero loaded the luggage. Climbing into the Cadillac's back seat, he settled in for the journey home.

***

Tuesday after school, Paul turned the jeep on their street, then pointed at a car in their driveway. "Isn't Mom home early from the office?"

Dan shaded his eyes as he looked. "Yeah. I hope nothing's wrong. Whose car is the other one?"

"Dunno. We must have company."

They stopped behind the navy blue sedan parked in front of their home. Hopping out of the jeep, Dan and Paul walked up to the door. As they did, a burst of laughter came from inside. The brothers exchanged puzzled glances as they opened the door.

Mrs. Case's voice called from the living room. "Boys? Is that you?"

"It's us, Mom," Paul answered.

The two stopped in their tracks when they entered the room. Their mother sat in the armchair, and a powerfully built man with black hair and sharp eyes, around their mother's age, occupied the couch. Both he and Mrs. Case were sipping coffee, appearing to get along very well. Paul and Dan recognized the man at once: Detective Barton from the Belmont Police Department. The twins had crossed paths with him when they all were involved in the protection racket gang case. Dan wondered what did he want with them now.

"We didn't do anything!" the twins said together.

Mrs. Case and Detective Barton laughed.

"We know you didn't," Mrs. Case said. "Steve just needs some information."

"Steve?" Paul asked under his breath.

Mrs. Case rose, putting her cup on the coffee table. "I have to get back to the office."

Detective Barton also got up. "Thank you for letting me wait here and for the coffee." He smiled. "It was very pleasant, Alice."

"Alice?" Paul murmured again. "What the—"

Mrs. Case smiled and picked up her purse. "My pleasure. We must do it again sometime."

"Yes, we should," Detective Barton returned the smile. "I would look forward to it."

"So would I," Mrs. Case said.

Paul gave a start. As their mother walked past the twins, she asked, "Who's making dinner tonight?"

Dan raised his hand. "I am. Paul has dirty dishes duty."

"Good. I'll be home around five-thirty. Bye, boys!" Mrs. Case went out the front door.

"Bye, Mom!" the brothers chorused.

Paul turned to Dan. "See? She said 'good' I was washing the dishes. I told you Mom thinks I do them better than you. She doesn't like the way you rinse them."

"She's just being polite," Dan said.

"Dan, I just have a few questions for you." The detective pulled out a notepad.

"Okay. Shoot." Dan jerked his thumb at his sibling. "Paul can stay, can't he?"

Barton nodded. "Sure. Were you out at the Maitland estate this past weekend?"

"Yes, Friday night and Saturday to about three in the afternoon," Dan answered. He added with pride, "Mrs. Maitland commissioned me to do a portrait."

"Of her dogs," Paul lobbed in.

Dan shot his brother a dirty look.

One of Barton's eyebrows shot up. "Dogs?"

"Max and Brutus," Dan said. "Her Great Danes."

"Oh. Anyway, when you were out there, did you notice anything unusual?" Detective Barton clicked his pen, ready to write.

Dan snorted. "You kidding? The whole joint is bananas."

Barton chuckled. "Specifically, did you note anything unusual about Andrew Maitland?"

Dan was surprised, but the detective's blank expression gave no further hints. He thought for a second and shook his head. "No."

Barton went on. "Well, did he seem anxious? Upset? Depressed?"

"Who could tell?" Dan shrugged. "The guy wears only one expression. I don't remember him saying anything like that, though."

"What's all this about, detective?" Paul asked.

Detective Barton closed his notepad with a flick of his wrist. "His mother filed a missing person report. Andrew Maitland has disappeared. "

Chapter Four

"You mean he's been kidnapped?" Paul asked.

Barton returned the pen and notepad to his coat pocket. "I'm not sure, Paul. I didn't find any indications you would expect in a kidnapping. No signs of foul play, a struggle, or evidence of forced entry. There hasn't been any contact for ransom, either." He shrugged. "But some of his clothes are gone. And his wallet, Mrs. Maitland confirmed."

"So he just went on an impromptu vacation?" Dan put in.

"I don't know about that, but he could have left home suddenly on his own accord. Dan, did there seem to be any trouble between Andrew and Mrs. Maitland?" the detective asked.

"You mean things like having arguments, or that sort of thing?" Dan thought for a moment, then shook his head. "No... I didn't notice that. Except she did ask him to stop talking about the Black Dahlia murder at breakfast..."

"The Black Dahlia murder?" Paul looked confused.

"It took place out in Los Angeles last year. The victim was severed in half at the waist, and completely drained of blood," Dan explained.

"Lovely. I guess that's a different topic of conversation than complaining the eggs are too runny," Paul said.

"So you didn't see anything? Anything at all?" Barton tried again.

"Well, I saw... or I thought I saw..." Dan's voice trailed off in an embarrassed mumble.

"What? What did you see?" the detective asked.

Dan wheeled on his brother and jabbed an index finger at him. "Don't you laugh at me!"

Paul held up his hands in surrender. "What? I wasn't laughing!"

"You were thinking about it!" Dan accused.

"Oh, what's the use," Paul groaned. He crossed his heart. "Cross my heart or hope to die, I promise not to do what I'm not doing when you tell us what you're not telling us."

"Okay." Dan took a deep breath. "Friday night, I thought I saw something prowling the halls of that place."

"Some*thing*?" Paul folded his arms and arched an eyebrow.

"Yes, *something*, dodo," Dan fired back. He faced the detective. "It was all in black and was wearing a robe. You know, like monks have on."

"Did you see, um, a face?" Barton asked.

Dan shook his head. "The cowl was up. One minute it was there, the next..." He snapped his fingers. "Poof! Gone! It was like a ghost." He added quietly, "Maybe it was."

Barton was silent for a moment. "Do you think this... whatever you saw, had any part in Andrew's disappearance?"

"I have no idea." Dan shivered. "All I know is, it was sure creepy."

"Well, so much for you going back to do your painting, Rembrandt," Paul said.

"Going back?" Barton looked at Dan.

"Yeah. I was supposed to return and stay at the estate during our spring break. To start the painting. You see, Mrs. Maitland wants it done plein aire." Dan noted Barton's puzzled expression. "It means done outside at the actual location, not in a studio or from a photo."

The detective nodded. He took a step toward Dan. "When will you know for sure if you'll be returning or not?"

"Day after tomorrow. Romero, the chauffeur, was going to call Thursday afternoon to arrange a time to pick me up," Dan said. He shrugged. "But with Andrew missing..."

"Look, guys, your help in the protection racket case was very important—" Barton started.

"I'd say the pictures my dear brother took were more than just important. They were vital," Paul said. "He caught all the gang in the act, including the leader."

"Alright, alright, you're correct. The photographs were critical, as were both of your depositions," the detective said. "I know the three of us butted heads at first, and I want to apologize for that."

"Thank you," Dan said. Paul nodded in acknowledgment.

"Now I'd like your help," Barton went on. "Dan, if you end up at the Maitland estate next week, keep your eyes peeled while you're there. Report anything unusual back to Paul, and he'll pass it on to me. I don't want anybody at the house to know you are, ah, 'helping' me. Would you do that?"

"Sure," Dan agreed.

"But remember, leave—" Barton began.

Paul tapped his brother on the shoulder and jerked a thumb toward the detective. "I bet he's going to tell you to leave the investigation work to him."

Barton shot an irritated glance at Paul. "Yes, that was exactly what I was going to say. And I mean it. I only need you to be an informant."

"Will do, Detective Barton," Dan said. He saluted. "Just call me Dan Case, junior G-Man."

***

Dan and Donna strolled hand in hand as they made their way to his house after the final school bell. Paul had taken the jeep for a job he had lined up that afternoon. The young couple finally arrived at the Case home.

"I'm sorry I can't ask you in, Donna. I'm being picked up in..." Dan checked his watch. "Wow. In like twenty minutes, and I haven't finished packing."

"So you'll be gone all next week? For the entire spring vacation?" Donna asked. "I was looking forward to spending some time with you. I was thinking about a picnic at the lake."

"I'll miss you too, but this commission is important to me. It's my first. I've sold some artwork before through the historical society, sure, but now I'm getting paid to paint a specific subject.

Somebody recognized me as an artist." Dan went on in almost a sheepish tone, "I mean, a real one."

"You are a real one. I predict this will be your first commission of many. I wish I could help you, though. Perhaps I could stand next to you and hand you brushes. You know, like a nurse hands instruments to a surgeon." Donna demonstrated.

Dan laughed. "You would be bored stiffer than my palette in five minutes." He thought for a moment. "But there is something you could do to help if you don't mind."

"Name it, handsome," Donna said.

"I've been wondering if Andrew's disappearance has any connection to his father, well, leaving the country so abruptly as it seems he did. It's weird they both pulled a vanishing act. Unless Andrew went after him." Dan shrugged. "Could you please look into it? Check the newspapers for stories. Andrew said Mr. Maitland left just before the war, so search editions from 1939, 1940, and 1941. Mr. Maitland was the head of a local company. His sudden departure must have warranted at least one news item."

"Alright." Donna counted on her fingers. "Maitland, Belmont Foundry — correct? — 1939 through 1941 — anything strange. Got it. I'll drag Betty along. The way Paul is working most days during the vacation, they're not going on any dates, anyway."

Dan grinned. "Thanks a lot. If you find any information, tell Paul. He'll let me know." He checked his watch and sucked in his breath. "Shoot! Ten minutes to finish packing! I've got to hightail it!" He and Donna exchanged a quick kiss. "I'll see you in a week!" he called as he ran into the house.

At the exact appointed time, the green Cadillac Fleetwood drew up in front of the house. Romero, as before, was courteous and reserved as he loaded Dan's easel, art supplies, and suitcase into the limo's spacious trunk. This time, Dan remembered the protocol and stood by the rear door until Romero opened it for him. He settled himself onto the comfortable backseat and waited for the chauffeur to close the door. The car pulled away from the curb and accelerated toward the Maitland estate.

"Everything quiet at the mansion?" Dan ventured after about ten minutes of silence.

"Quiet as a crypt, sir," Romero answered. In the rearview mirror, Dan met his gaze—one that held a hint of suspicion. Dan shifted his position to look out the window for the rest of the drive.

Dan hopped out of the rear seat as soon as Romero opened the door after the limo stopped at the front of the Maitlands' house. He followed the chauffeur through the grand entrance and into the foyer. Mrs. Maitland was fussing over a vase of daffodils on a small table.

"Hello, Mrs. Maitland," Dan said as he entered. She acted awfully calm for someone who just filed a missing person report, he thought.

"Daniel! A pleasure to see you again!" Mrs. Maitland smiled as she approached Dan. She clasped her hands together and leaned toward him. "Are you ready to begin making your artistic magic?"

"Yes." Dan gestured to Romero, who was carrying his art supplies up to the guest room. "I brought all the tools of my trade!"

Max and Brutus bounded into the foyer, their large paws tapping against the stone floors. They immediately made a beeline for Dan, who was standing in the center of the room. Familiar with their welcoming routine, he braced himself as the Great Danes playfully nuzzled and begged for attention.

Dan laughed. "I guess my subjects are ready." He scratched the dogs behind their ears. He kept his eyes on Mrs. Maitland as he asked his next question. "Is Andrew around?"

"Oh, that son of mine! He can be such a trial!" Her hands fluttered by her head, her silver hair catching the light as she turned. "He's always off somewhere. It was Palm Springs last month. Now it's off to Santa Anita Park in California. It's horse racing season out there. Can you believe it? He didn't even tell me he was going before he left. I only found his note two days later! Such a naughty boy. I'll have to give him a good talking to."

"Naughty indeed," Dan said to himself. A spontaneous trip to the races or a convenient alibi? Or did she jump the gun and file the missing person report too soon? He was wondering how he could discover that when Mrs. Maitland spoke.

"Dinner is at seven," she announced. "I'll leave you to get settled in."

"I'd like to explore the rest of the estate, actually," Dan said.

Mrs. Maitland made a sweeping gesture. "Of course! I'll see you tonight."

Dan stepped outside, with Max and Brutus following closely behind. He surveyed his surroundings before deciding to investigate the crypt first. As he walked there, a strange prickling sensation crawled up the back of his neck. Someone was watching him.

He spun around, scanning the impressive mansion in back of him. For a brief moment, he thought he saw a figure at the second-floor window, then it disappeared like a ghostly apparition. Dan squinted. Was it real or just a trick of the light?

"A reflection of some sort," he reassured himself. "Besides, ghosts don't walk during the day. Unless their watch is broken."

The crypt certainly fit the part. It was gothic in style, with spires and pillars. The walls were constructed from sturdy blocks of stone, and the roof was slate tiles. Engraved above an arched doorway was the name "Collins". Dan grasped the handle and pushed open the elaborate wrought-iron gate that acted as a door, stepping into the gloomy interior. The faint sunlight filtering through small windows created eerie patterns on the floor. As his eyes adjusted to the dimness, Dan surveyed the room. It certainly appeared to be a burial vault, with low shelves lining two walls that would have held caskets but were currently empty.

When he stepped out of the cold building, the dogs were playing on the lawn. Dan let them be and headed towards the canal.

The tranquil waterway was roughly twenty feet across, bordered by solid stones. Bushes grew right up to the edge and drooped over the sides. The sun's rays danced on the surface, creating a twinkling display of light and shadow. As he took in the scene, a thirty-foot power cabin cruiser motored by on its way from the river to the lake. Dan was retracing his path when Max and Brutus bounded up to him.

"Hey, guys! Did you just realize I left you?" Dan asked, rubbing behind the dog's ears. That's when he noticed a piece of paper tucked into Max's collar. Plucking it out, he unfolded it. His brow furrowed as he read the cryptic words typed on the half-sheet of paper: "Enter the hedge maze if you dare but be warned: not all who wander find their way back. The twisting paths conceal secrets. Step lightly, for each turn might lead to wonders untold or to shadows that whisper your name."

Dan chuckled nervously as his eyes darted around the area. A mysterious, anonymous message. But what else could he expect at a house that resembled a castle, complete with a crypt and a dungeon? Since somebody had taken some trouble to send the note by canine express, he should follow up on it.

After tucking the note into his back pocket, Dan made his way towards the green walls of the maze. The hedges were roughly seven feet in height, towering over him as he stood at the entrance. He hesitated a moment, not wanting to become lost inside. Then he remembered a trick his dad had taught the brothers when they went to an amusement park fun house: always turn in one direction.

He cast a quick glance over his shoulder, but Max and Brutus were off romping somewhere. "Thanks for the backup, guys."

Taking a deep breath, Dan entered the maze, keeping his hand brushing against the tall hedge on his right. As he moved deeper into the twisted pathways, the air grew colder, the shadows darker, and the silence heavier. By the third corner, he realized the note didn't tell him what he would find. The last time he saw Andrew, he was going in here... it couldn't be that stumbling over his corpse would be the "wonders untold"?

"Happy thought," he said under his breath.

At last, he finally reached the heart of the maze. A sturdy gate made of wood stood out in stark contrast against the surrounding greenery. The ground in front of the gate was disturbed, as well as a few broken, thin branches. It seemed as if there had been a struggle there. He cautiously pushed open the gate and entered into a small clearing, enclosed by tall hedges on all sides.

In the center rested a chest made of white wood, looking like a casket. The earth by it was also scuffed up. Dan cautiously approached the box, wondering what was inside.

"Andrew?" Dan said as he lifted the lid. "Are you in there?"

There was nothing in the box but a few garden tools. Closing the top, he spotted another piece of paper, wedged against the base of a hedge, partially covered in dirt. He got on his knees, snatched it, and stood.

The note appeared to have been out in the elements for several days, weeks perhaps, judging by its crinkled and dirty appearance. Dan gingerly unfolded it and read the typed message: "Come to the maze at 3:30, if you want to learn something beneficial."

Dan slipped the message into his pocket, thinking about its contents. He couldn't help but wonder if this was the same letter he had seen Andrew pull from the pile of mail last Saturday morning. He remembered seeing the younger Maitland walk towards the hedges when Dan left the estate at about 3:00 PM that day. Was Andrew headed to this meeting mentioned in the note? And could it have something to do with his sudden disappearance? Indeed, had he disappeared at all, but instead went to California like Mrs. Maitland said? Was she lying? Before Dan could contemplate his next move, a rough voice shattered the silent tension.

"You! What are you doing here? This area is off-limits!"

Dan spun around to face a man who appeared at the gate like a ferocious troll guarding a bridge. In his sixties, the man was dressed in faded jeans and a worn, long-sleeve plaid shirt. A few strands of snow-white hair peeked out from under his floppy hat, adding to his gruff appearance.

"You must be Mr. Lang, the gardener," Dan said with what he hoped was a friendly smile.

"What of it?" Lang growled.

"I'm Dan Case. Mrs. Maitland has commissioned me to do a painting—"

"In here?" Lang squinted with one eye as he stared at Dan in undisguised annoyance. All he needed was a parrot on his shoulder to resemble a pirate.

Dan laughed. Lang glared. "No, of course not. I was just looking around the estate. Were you doing some work in the maze?"

"No, it was time for my coffee break!" Lang spat back. "I was transplanting, if that meets with your lordship's approval."

Dan gave a brief look at the gardener. Despite Lang's hands being calloused from years of hard labor, they were spotless. His jeans also showed no signs of dirt or grime. When Paul came back from transplanting in a client's garden, his hands would be dirty even if he wore gloves, and his pants would be covered in soil, particularly around the knees. Then Dan noticed the glint of something gold peeking from beneath the gardener's sleeve—a watch that seemed far too opulent for someone whose days were spent wrestling with weeds and wrangling rose bushes.

"Oh, transplanting... Sorry, you're not holding a trowel. You must have left it back where you were working," Dan said.

"Get out of here before you trample something important," the gardener snapped, waving Dan off.

"Of course, Mr. Lang. I don't want to get in your way," Dan said.

As he made his way out of the hedges, Dan's mind was flooded with questions about the mysterious house and its strange inhabitants. Who had sent him the cryptic message directing him to the maze? Was it the same individual — or thing — he saw on his first night here? And why direct him to that spot in the first place, especially if Andrew's reason for being away was simply to attend horse races in California?

But that second note he found suggested something else, something sinister, perhaps, was occurring. Was Mrs. Maitland hiding something about her son's whereabouts? Was this more than a missing person case and potentially a kidnapping, after all?

Dan was relieved when he emerged from the hedges into the open air and sunshine. Barton would have to figure out the mystery of the messages — after all, Dan was just an informant, as the detective had so explicitly pointed out. He headed for the mansion.

"Mrs. Danner, may I use the phone?" Dan asked as he stepped into the kitchen.

"Surely." She wiped her hands on her apron as she led him to a telephone sitting on a mahogany table in the hall. Dan picked up the receiver. The housekeeper moved a few steps away and stopped.

Dan smiled. "Thank you."

Mrs. Danner took another few steps, still lingering in the hallway.

"Thank you," Dan repeated. "I've got it."

Throwing a suspicious glance at Dan, Mrs. Danner shuffled back to the kitchen. When he was alone, Dan dialed. Waiting for the call to be completed, he glanced at the portraits lining the halls. They all seemed to be staring directly at him. "Mind your own business," he muttered to the painted images.

"Case residence." His brother's voice was a welcome sound.

"Hi, buddy, it's me," Dan said. "Listen, can you—"

A click on the line cut him short. Someone had picked up an extension and was eavesdropping.

"Dan?"

"Yeah, still here, sorry. I got distracted. Can you do a favor for me? Could you bring me a tube of paint I forgot?" Dan glanced around the hall.

"One tube of paint? Aw, Danny boy, come on, don't you have enough pretty pastels in your little box?" Paul groused.

"I need to have a specific one," Dan said with emphasis.

"Can't you substitute some other? I mean, for crying out loud, to drive all the way out there to—" his twin started.

"Paul, I know it's a lot to ask, but it's very important. Vital, in fact," Dan stressed.

Paul sighed. "Alright, alright, I'll do it, but you owe me one, my dear brother. What do you need, Rembrandt?"

"It's in the order I got on Tuesday afternoon. The color is Barton Blue." Dan pronounced the name carefully.

There was a slight pause. "Got it," Paul replied, the unspoken understanding clear in his tone. "I'll be there tomorrow."

"Thanks, buddy, I appreciate it. See you then." Dan held on after Paul hung up, listening. He heard a faint click as the extension phone was put down.

Chapter Five

D an dabbed his brush onto the palette, his eyes squinting in concentration at the canvas.

"Look," came a hushed voice from behind him, "he's about to paint!"

"Yes!" whispered a second woman. "Isn't it thrilling?"

Mrs. Maitland's bridge club, a gaggle of genteel women, clustered behind Dan, watching him as though he was a trained monkey performing at the circus. He closed his eyes and took a deep breath, trying to ignore them. He added the color on the canvas.

"Dear, isn't that rose bush just a tad too... purple?" a third member of the audience questioned.

Dan added another defiant stroke. He turned to face the ladies and forced a smile. "Artistic license. The artist's keen eye sees beyond the surface of life, delving into a world of imagination and creation. Our perception transcends reality, painting a unique and vivid depiction of the surrounding environment."

He had no idea of the meaning of what he just said, but it satisfied his audience, anyway. They murmured in approval as they nodded their heads in agreement.

"Quite avant-garde," another cooed, her voice dripping with enough syrup to give a hummingbird diabetes.

"Well, ladies, we need to let Daniel continue to pursue his artistic vision," Mrs. Mailtand said. "We have a rubber of bridge that requires our attention!"

The bridge players fluttered toward the mansion, chattering, while their perfume lingered in the air like a nosy ghost. Dan rolled his eyes and turned back to the painting. He lost track of how long he worked before somebody interrupted his concentration again by talking behind him.

"I'm not really sure about that sky color."

Dan spun around on his stool and, with a deft flick of his brush, gave his brother a cobalt blue Hitler mustache.

"Hey!" Paul grabbed Dan's paint rag and scrubbed off the offending mark.

Standing next to Paul was a lanky teen with a wild mass of blonde hair. Jake wasn't just Paul's sparring partner, he was also connected to the protection racket gang the brothers had taken down in October. After realizing his error in serving as their lookout, Jake provided Paul with a crucial piece of information that led to the gang's capture.

"Hi, Jake!" Dan said. He pointed at his brother with his brush. "Why are you hanging around with that loser?"

"I'm his newest employee." Jake took in the estate and hooked his thumbs into his jeans pockets and gave a low whistle of approval. "Although this joint doesn't look half bad a place to work and hang your hat. Better than the dump my Ma and I live in."

"I'll put a good word in for you to Mrs. Maitland," Dan grinned.

Paul dropped the rag on Dan's paint box. "I had a big job today. Needed to clear an overgrown garden, so I added Jake to the payroll."

Max and Brutus galloped up to Dan and stood at his side, staring at the newcomers. Paul and Jake gasped and instinctively took a step back from the beasts.

Paul pointed at the dogs. "Do those things come with saddles?"

Dan laughed and patted the Great Danes. They sat at his feet. "This is Max, and this is Brutus. Don't let their size intimidate you."

"Me, intimidated? By a couple of pooches! Never!" Paul said. There was a slight, uncomfortable pause. "They have been fed, haven't they?" He relaxed after Dan nodded. "Pleased to meet you both, fellows... I think." He saluted the dogs, then pulled a tube out of his pocket. "Oh, here's that color you needed, Rembrandt."

"Thanks." Dan took the paint, waving it in such a way it was visible to any onlookers. As he placed it with his other paints, he spoke out of the corner of his mouth, "I think I'm being watched and listened to."

"What's all this about? Who's watching you?" Jake blurted out.

Paul reacted as if Jake had just told a wild joke. He clapped Jake on the back and said through his hearty laughter, "Laugh and shut up." After a confused second, Jake did so. Paul continued in a quiet voice to his twin. "Was that the reason for this business with needing that paint?"

Dan nodded.

"Who is behind it?" Paul asked.

Dan clamped his brother around his shoulder and pulled him close. He made a sweeping gesture encompassing the mansion as though showing it off to Paul, speaking while smiling at the same time. "Don't know. The place is loaded with suspects. It could be Mrs. Maitland or Mrs. Danner... she's the housekeeper." Keeping his eyes forward, he jerked his head in the chauffeur's direction, washing the Cadillac in front of the carriage house. He stared at them as he wrung out a large sponge. "Romero or..." another tilt of the head toward the gardener pruning some rose bushes, "Lang. Or person or persons unknown."

Paul watched Lang for a moment and snorted. "That guy's a gardener?"

Dan sat on his stool and started pointing things out on his painting to his brother. "Why do you say that?"

Paul leaned over Dan's shoulder to inspect the art and spoke into Dan's ear. "Because he doesn't know how to prune. Mrs. Carmichael would kill me if I whacked her roses like that!"

"Are you sure?"

"Easy enough to find out." Paul straightened up and strode over to Lang. "Hey there, how are you doing?"

Lang grunted an answer.

Paul tapped himself on his chest. "I do landscaping, too."

"I'm happy for ya," Lang grumbled.

"Say, I've got a problem with one of my client's alopecia," Paul said. "How do you handle those beauties?"

Paul winced as Lang clipped another innocent bloom. The gardener looked up. When he replied, his voice held the certainty of a man used to being believed. "Water twice daily at dawn and dusk," he declared.

"Much obliged! I'll try that!" Paul said and headed back to Dan with a smirk. He gave a slight nod of his head toward the jeep. He spoke loudly to make sure he was overheard. "Well, my dear brother, we've got to go. I'll let you slave over a hot paintbrush."

The three boys casually walked in the direction of the front driveway. Max and Brutus tagged along. Lang kept a suspicious eye on them from behind the rose bushes.

"Well? What did you find out?" Dan asked when they reached the jeep.

"That Lang is a phony." Paul climbed behind the wheel. "I asked him about alopecia, and he told me to water it twice daily."

"What's alopecia?" Jake asked as he settled into the passenger seat.

"Baldness," Paul replied. "That's not botany. And that guy Lang's no gardener."

"He should know about being bald. I think he's wearing a rug," Jake said.

Dan turned to Jake. "A rug?"

"Yeah. You know, a rug, a wig, a... a... toupee. Yeah, that's the fancy word. Toupee," Jake patted the top of his head. "My old man wore one. Left it behind when he scrammed out on Ma and me. I can spot them a mile away."

Dan gave a sigh. "Just what I need — another mystery in this crazy place."

"Are you safe here, buddy? You're not in any danger, are you?" Paul asked.

"No, everything's okay. It's just creepy, that's all," Dan answered.

Paul tossed a quick glance around to make certain they were alone. "What about Andrew?"

"Mrs. Maitland said he went to California, but I'm not so sure. I'm sure Barton doesn't think so, either." Dan pulled the notes out of his pocket and slipped them to Paul. "Show him those. I've added some information on my own. Let me know what he says."

"If you're being listened to, I won't call. Jake or I will come out," Paul said.

Dan nodded. He stepped back from the jeep and checked his watch. He exclaimed. "Well, I can get in another hour until the light shifts. I'd better get back to it. Thanks for bringing that paint, Paul. I appreciate it! See you, Jake!"

"Bye, Dan. Don't work too hard!" Paul called back as he started the engine.

***

Dan gave a last wave before heading back to his easel, trailed by the dogs. Paul passed the papers to Jake, speaking out of the corner of his mouth. "Put those in the toolbox back there." Jake turned to the rear seat. "Don't be so obvious, man!"

"Oh." Jake sat facing forward and reached behind himself to open the metal box. He opened it with one hand, and slipped the notes inside, then closed it.

Paul wheeled the jeep down the drive.

As they drove away, Jake leaned over to speak to Paul. "Did Dan say Barton? Like in Detective Barton?"

"Mrs. Maitland filed a missing person report on her son, Andrew. That's on the QT, by the way." Paul stopped the jeep at the end of the driveway, checking the cross traffic. "Barton asked Dan to keep an eye out when he's here."

Paul eased out from the Maitland estate onto the road. They had driven almost to the bridge crossing the river when a sleek black sedan zoomed past them.

"Idiot! Watch out!" the deafening roar of the sedan's engine drowned Paul's words out as it swerved around a curve, lost control, and plunged off the road into the water below. Paul slammed on the brakes, the jeep skidding to a stop.

"Jake, go get help!" Paul leaped out of the driver's seat.

The sound of the jeep faded into the distance as Paul raced down to the river bank, tossing his glasses and shirt aside before plunging into the dark water. He swam towards the overturned car and gripped the door handle, twisting it with all his might. His lungs burned for air as he worked faster, desperation driving him to save whoever was inside.

A hand grasped his own and a frantic struggle ensued as the trapped driver clawed at him, fighting for survival. Paul fought off the panicked man climbing up his shoulders, bubbles bursting from their lips as they used up precious oxygen in their fight for life.

The man's grip on Paul's hand was loose. Paul slipped out of the grasp but wrapped his arm under the driver's arms. Using the car as leverage, Paul pushed off and propelled them both upwards towards the sun. Gasping for air, he hauled the man out of the water and onto the bank, their bodies soaked.

With the thought that there may be others still stuck inside the vehicle, Paul plunged into the river once more. He kicked his feet and descended to the submerged car, feeling around on the seats and floor. Finding nobody else, he returned to the surface.

Back on dry land, the driver lay on his back, sputtering and coughing, one arm laying over his eyes. Paul removed the guy's coat, folding it to cushion his head. The driver moved his arm, his eyes locked onto Paul's dripping face, and he gasped, "It's you!" He jumped up and sprinted away like a scared rabbit.

"Hey!" Paul stood and yelled, but the man was long gone. Shaking his head, he said to himself, "What the heck was that all about?"

Paul got back on his knees and rummaged through the abandoned coat, hoping to find some kind of identification. He pulled out a wet envelope. Carefully peeling it apart, he extracted a photostat of a ledger page, accompanied by a typewritten note that read, "This is only a sample. The price will go up. Decide."

Chapter Six

After working another couple of hours on details, Dan packed away his easel and supplies. He wondered what Barton's reaction would be when Paul showed him the messages. It would be interesting to find out.

Carrying everything to his room, he paused to gaze at the half-finished painting. It was shaping up well, he reassured himself. With a satisfied smile, he went downstairs and headed to the kitchen. The sound of chatter and laughing drifted from behind the closed living room doors. The bridge game must still be going strong. Mrs. Danner was arranging some deviled eggs on a tray when Dan entered.

"Could I have a glass of milk, please?" he asked. "When you have time."

"Certainly. I think we have some," Mrs. Danner answered. "Help yourself. Glasses are in the top left cupboard."

A burst of laughter came from the bridge club. Dan gestured toward the voices. "It sounds like quite a game."

Mrs. Danner picked up the tray. "It's more a gossiping hen party than playing cards, I think." She bustled out of the swinging door.

Dan chuckled and opened the cabinet. As he reached in to grab a glass, he noticed a sheaf of papers tacked to the inside of the door. The heading read "Dietary Treatment of a Peptic Ulcer". The list contained recommendations like a bland diet, frequent small meals, and easily digested foods. A sample menu was given: "Breakfast: oatmeal with milk, toast with a small amount of butter, and a glass of milk. Mid-Morning Snack: A small serving of cottage cheese or a glass of milk. Lunch: Boiled chicken, mashed potatoes, cooked carrots, and a glass of milk."

"That's bland, alright," Dan said.

Mrs. Danner's voice startled him. "That was for Mr. Maitland."

Dan spun around. "I'm sorry. I didn't mean to pry. It was just hanging there…"

The housekeeper shrugged. "No harm done. The poor man suffered from a stomach ulcer. I don't know why I haven't taken it down since he… left." She held out a hand. "Here, let me get your milk."

"Thank you." Dan gave her the glass. He tilted his head toward the paper. "Was it because of stress, or…"

"He developed it from running the foundry. That's what I say." Mrs. Danner pulled a bottle of milk from the refrigerator and poured a glassful. "Mr. Maitland was smart at tinkering. Invented a machine and got one of those fancy patents for it. It's used by foundries all over. He loved things like that. He always spent time on the floor, trying to refine this or that process."

Dan chuckled as he took the full glass from Mrs. Danner. He noticed her puzzled expression. "Oh, I thought that was a joke. 'Refine'... at a foundry... you know, casting metals... refine..."

Mrs. Danner smiled. "I didn't mean that, sir! The foundry grew, but Mr. Maitland was, well, he was just terrible at the business end. That's what I say. Actually running the place, day to day. Things like taxes, payroll, bookkeeping, and contracts. He was disorganized, forgetful... he worried himself into that ulcer about them."

"Was Andrew involved at all? Maybe a part-time job there?" Dan took a drink of milk.

She gave a derisive laugh and wave of one hand. "Not him! He couldn't be bothered. Interfered with his party going. Or throwing away money at the horse races."

"Well, Mr. Maitland did well, even if he was disorganized." Dan's sweeping gesture took in the estate.

"That's due to Mr. Dietz," the cook said. "Mr. Maitland finally hired Mr. Dietz to handle all of those affairs. That man never met a column of figures he didn't like. Kept records of everything, and I mean everything. He was exactly who Mr. Maitland needed. Dietz handled the accounts and paperwork, while Maitland ran the actual foundry. It went so smoothly that Mr. Maitland made Mr. Dietz a partner. The foundry was successful and boomed for years until..."

A brief look of sadness crossed the housekeeper's face. She turned and busied herself at the counter. Dan sipped the milk, waiting for Mrs. Danner to continue. After a few moments, it was clear she wouldn't. "How long have you worked for the Maitlands?"

"Ten years I've been with them," Mrs. Danner said with pride. "Through thick and thin. And there's been a lot of thick."

"Romero and Lang haven't been here nearly as long, have they?" Dan leaned against the counter as he took another drink of milk.

"Romero's a flash in the pan. Here only two months. About the same number of words I've gotten out of him, too," she sniffed. "And Lang, about six. That man should be grateful to have a gardener's cottage, right here on the property, and not just a room, like the rest of us. But no. Instead, he holes up at the Colony Hotel in town. All high and mighty like, like some hot shot traveling salesman. He's lucky Mrs. Mailtand doesn't pay that much attention to the grounds. As long as they're green, that's fine with her. That's what I say."

"Seems like there's a lot of turnover around here," Dan said.

"We can't even keep a maid. We use an agency to clean the house. Mrs. Maitland isn't easy to please," Mrs. Danners confided. She leaned toward Dan and gave a wink. "Except I know how to handle her. Others don't have my patience."

Dan drained his glass. "Thanks for the milk," he said. And the information, he thought.

***

Paul's still-damp sneakers squeaked against the linoleum as he strode into the lobby at the Belmont Police Station, holding the soggy ledger sample and Dan's notes. He approached the front desk.

"Is Detective Barton around?" Paul asked, pushing up the bridge of his glasses.

"Out of town, testifying in a case," grumbled the officer on duty, barely looking up from his crossword puzzle. He reached for a glazed doughnut resting on a paper towel. "Should be back Monday or Tuesday."

"Okay, thanks," said Paul. "I'll check back then. Nothing important."

Yeah, right, he thought. He had possible clues burning a hole in his pocket and no detective to give them to, but he couldn't do anything about that. He checked his watch. Just enough time to do his chores at home and grab a shower before picking up Betty for their date.

Later that night, the two broke from an embrace as they stood on Betty's front porch.

"That was my favorite part of the movie," Paul said.

"There wasn't a scene like this in the picture," Betty smiled back.

"Should have been." Paul leaned in for another kiss.

The outdoor light snapped on.

Betty gave an eye-roll. "My father's subtle suggestion. Time to come inside."

Paul grinned. "Understood. Well, I have to be getting home, too."

"Oh, Donna and I have some dope on Mr. Maitland. We're going to call Dan tomorrow," Betty said.

Paul remembered what Dan had told him about being watched. It worried him a little, but he didn't want Betty to know that. "It would be better to see him in person. He's working outside... on the tennis court. He's not near a phone."

"Alright, we'll pop out," Betty said. "Do you want to tag along?"

Paul shook his head. "I've got a couple of lawns to mow after church. There are storms in the forecast for this week. I need to squeeze jobs in before it starts to rain. Oh, try getting up to the Maitland house after two. That sounds like when Dan quits painting because the light changes or he turns into a pumpkin or something." He turned toward the front door and waved. "Good night, Mr. Wilson."

After another quick kiss, Paul drove home. Mrs. Case sat in the living room, reading a magazine, when he walked in.

"How was the movie?" she asked.

"Great."

Paul's mom cocked one eyebrow as she asked the next question. "What was the title?"

"Title?"

"Of the picture."

"'I was a Male War Bride,'" Paul answered with the confidence of a student over-prepared for a test. "Starred Cary Grant."

Mrs. Case gave a knowing smile. "I'm glad you paid attention to the movie."

"Of course I did, Mom!" Paul said. Mostly, he thought. "Good night."

"Night, dear."

When he stepped into his room, he gave a slight shiver. The room was chilly, and then he saw why. The window stood wide open, the curtains flirting with the night breeze.

Paul knew he had closed that when he left. He glanced at his desk, where he had placed the notes from Dan and the paper from the accident before heading to the movies. The desktop was bare.

***

After dinner, Mrs. Mailand and Dan went again to the living room to watch television. Dan sat on the couch, leaning toward the screen, as the final note of the Texaco Star Theater theme music sounded from the TV.

"That Milton Bearle is a scream! So funny!" Mrs. Maitland got up from her chair. "But now it is time for bed."

"Do you mind if I stayed up and watched some more television?" Dan asked shyly, almost as though doing so would break the magic box.

Mrs. Maitland laughed. "Why, of course, you may, Daniel! Goodnight." She floated out of the room.

"Night," Dan said, his gaze already wandering back to the TV.

His eyes remained glued to the screen, absorbing every flickering image and tinny sound. He remained transfixed until the broadcasting station finally signed off for the night, leaving behind a harsh static test pattern on the once-vibrant screen. Slowly, he blinked and stretched, the room around him quiet and still. He checked the clock: 11:00 pm. Standing, he stretched, reached over, and switched off the set.

He froze. Framed in the living room doorway behind him, reflected on the darkened television screen, was the cloaked figure.

Chapter Seven

Dan's heart raced as he stared at the indistinct figure reflected in the darkened television screen, cloaked in a monk's robe, with its face hidden deep beneath the cowl. Dan closed his eyes, hoping the image was just a figment of his imagination, or some type of weird, electronic leftover from the TV set. But when he reopened his eyes, the thing was still there. It glided out of the doorway without making a sound. Dan swallowed hard.

"Okay, Dan... there are no such things as ghosts... there are no such things as ghosts," he chanted under his breath, then gave a shaky exhalation. "Even if they do exist, ghosts don't have reflections. No, wait, that's vampires. Isn't it? So, anyway, it's time to do some ghost hunting."

He turned around. His feet didn't want to move forward. He forced them to and tiptoed towards the doorway. An old floorboard creaked, sounding like a gunshot in the silence. Why do they always do that at night?

Taking tentative steps, he entered the dark hallway. It ran down the center of the house and had no windows, so the only source of light was the faint glow coming from the lamp in the living room behind him, casting sharp and grotesque shadows on the wall opposite the door. Inky blackness shrouded everything else down the hall, leaving the impression of a hungry, gaping maw.

Despite the ice water running down his spine and the urge to flee back to the safety of the brightly lit room, Dan stayed put. He wasn't afraid *of* the dark, he told himself. He was afraid of just what could be hiding *in* the dark. His eyes darted around, searching for any sign of movement from the lurking figure.

At that moment, he thought turning on the lights would be the smartest choice. This was the twentieth century, after all. No need to stumble in darkness like a terrified peasant from the 1500s. Then he realized he had no clue where the switch was. Fumbling around in the blackness wouldn't be smart and would call attention to his location. He needed to pack a flashlight at all times in this place.

With quiet steps, Dan moved forward. Memories of movies he'd watched where characters ventured precisely into places they clearly shouldn't, like old graveyards and creepy basements, filled his mind. Like any audience member with common sense, he was positive that this was a stupid idea.

So here he was, following something unknown down a dark hallway.

Dan felt his way along the wall with the tips of his fingers. He paused, straining for any sound that wasn't his own breathing—which was loud enough, he was sure, to wake the dead. Or at least alert them to his presence, to a living, warm-blooded, decidedly non-ghostly intruder.

The library doors were shut tight. He didn't hear them open-ing, so the mysterious figure mustn't have used them. Then again, ghosts had little need for proper door usage. They floated through them.

Stop it, he scolded himself.

Dan's breath hitched as a shadowy form detached from the darkness, darker than the inky blackness swallowing the sur-rounding space. It moved with an eerie silence, gliding into the dining room like a whisper against silk. For a moment, Dan's feet rooted to the spot, his heart thudding in his ears. Cautiously following, he approached the entrance of the dining room and peered inside.

The moonlight filtering through the windows sliced the floor into white rectangles. The mounted animals on the walls seemed to be lurking, waiting, their lifeless glass eyes staring at him as he stepped into the room. A soft rustling noise broke through the stillness, making Dan wonder if the ferocious boar head was getting ready to attack.

The sound came from the other side of the swinging door. He pushed his way through.

The blueish-white light from the moon also sterilized the kitchen. The razor-sharp blades of Mrs. Danner's knives hanging on the wall gleamed on their own. Dan crept to the back door.

The knob was locked, and the interior sliding bolt was in place. The mysterious figure hadn't exited the house here unless it somehow could slip an inside bolt from the outside. But where had it gone?

Of course, if it was a ghost, it did what all self-respecting spirits do. It vanished... caught the last bus back to its grave or the afterlife waiting room or wherever. He shook his head. Stop thinking that way.

His eyes darted to a glimmer of light escaping from under a door on the other side of the room. He paused for a moment, then made his way towards it.

As he opened the door, he stepped into a narrow hallway with five doors on the left and one at the far end. Its plainness was out of place compared to the rest of the lavish house. This must have been built for the servants' quarters.

The first door in the hall was closed, but a soft cadence of breathing told him it wasn't empty. He guessed it was Mrs. Danner. The next room was open, revealing an unoccupied space furnished with a simple bed, dresser, and chair.

The door was ajar in the third room, a dim light coming from a bedside lamp. Dan peeked in. Personal items, like combs and brushes, lay scattered on the bureau. A paperback book rested on the nightstand, and there, tossed atop the bed, was a piece of dark material. Perhaps it was the monk's habit of belonging to the figure haunting this house. It looked like it, but Dan couldn't be sure. He leaned through the doorway for a closer peek.

"Mr. Case, may I help you?" a voice cut through the silence, as gruff and startling as an engine backfiring.

Dan's breath caught as he whirled around. Romero, dressed simply in pajama bottoms, stood behind him like a Greek statue brought to life. His imposing physique radiated strength and menace. A towel was draped over one shoulder, while one hand held a toothbrush like it was a minty-fresh scepter. The next door down was open, revealing the tiled wall of the bathroom.

"Uh, hi, Romero." Dan squeaked. He cleared his throat to get his pitch to sound normal again. "I was just, uh, looking for a drink of water. You know, I always say water from the kitchen faucet tastes better than from the bathroom faucet." His laugh was so weak it needed crutches. "Don't you think so?"

Romero's expression suggested he found the humor not particularly amusing.

"I guess you don't. Well, yes sir, that's what I always say." Dan gave a halfhearted punch in the air for emphasis and forced a grin.

"You are in the wrong place, Mr. Case," Romero said, the unyielding tone of his voice suggesting he was not in the habit of repeating himself.

"Right, wrong, of course. My mistake." Dan backed away with his hands held up in surrender. He circled one index finger in the air. "Got turned around. In the dark."

"If I hadn't recognized you, sir, the results could have been most unpleasant." Romero's glare could have pulverized Dan by itself.

"Yes... well, sorry. I, ah, ah, 'I knew I should've taken that left turn at Albuquerque!' Ha ha. That's what Bugs Bunny always says. In... in the cartoons. 'I knew I should've taken that left turn at Albuquerque!' You know..." Dan did his best impression of the character, "'eh, what's up, doc?' Him."

Romero's stern expression didn't change.

"Well, no reason to hang around all night. You probably want to prowl around... ah, get to bed now. I'll... ah... I'll get my water now." Dan pointed to the kitchen, then quickly left the hall, half expecting a knife in his back.

He drank a glass of water, even though he didn't really want it, but he had to back up his story. Hurrying to his room, he found Max and Brutus sprawled on the floor. They looked up when Dan came in and thumped their tails. "Where were you two when I needed you?"

Dan sat on the bed, thinking as he started to untie his shoes. Was Romero the mysterious figure in the monk's habit? The chauffeur was the same height, and the trail appeared to lead to his room... The material he saw in his room *could* have been the monk's robe, but he wasn't sure.

He should have asked — no, demanded — Romero let him examine the garment. He shook his head at the stupidity of the idea. Who was he kidding? He recalled Romero's veiled threat. And with biceps like the chauffeur's, Dan could easily have been hammered into the floor like a nail.

"Drove a general around Italy, huh?" Dan pulled off one shoe. That glare Romero gave him was from somebody who may have served as a deadly operative in the Office of Strategic Services during the war. Assassin, maybe. But not a driver to some brass.

He took off his other sneaker and also dropped it next to the other one. But why? Why the costume? Why creep through the house at night? Did it have anything to do with Andrew vanishing? And was it a "disappearance" in the first place? What about the weird note? If Romero wasn't the monk, who was? Or what was it?

With a frustrated "bah", he got up to finish getting ready for bed. None of what was going on in this loony bin made any sense.

***

The following afternoon couldn't be more different from the shadow-laden encounters of the previous night. The sunshine cheered Dan up and was actually smiling while he painted. The artwork was coming together better than he expected. The placement of Max and Brutus fit the composition just as he wanted, and he worked briskly, filling in details, going light to dark, light to dark parts of the art.

Around two o'clock, a burst of giggling came from behind him, breaking his concentration. "They're so cute!" came two voices.

Dan swiveled on his stool, his eyes drawn to the sight of Donna and Betty fawning over Max and Brutus. The two large dogs were lapping up the attention, their tails wagging with so much excitement they might take flight at any moment.

Betty cupped Max's face in her hands and cooed. "Who's a good boy? You're a good boy! Such a good boy!"

Max tried to lick her face.

"You're spoiling them," Dan warned.

"Too late!" Donna walked over to Dan, her auburn hair catching the light as she gave him a quick peck on the cheek. She put her hands on Dan's shoulders and leaned over to look at the painting. Betty joined them. "That's excellent, handsome!"

"Thanks," Dan said, blushing a hue that rivaled her hair. He always did when she called him "handsome" in front of others.

"That is wonderful, Dan!" Betty chimed in as she viewed the art. "When will you be finished?"

"It won't take too long." Dan gestured over the painting with his brush. "Depends on how many details I add."

"Oh, Paul phoned. He wanted me to tell you the notes were taken," Betty said.

Dan sat up straight. "Taken? What did he mean?"

Betty shrugged. "He didn't say anything else. Just said he wanted you to know."

"That's interesting," Dan glanced around. He didn't want to be overheard.

"We've been digging up dirt on Maitland and boy, we have news for you!" Donna said.

"Great... but don't tell me here," Dan said, holding out a cautioning hand. "Let's grab some lunch in town. How does that sound?"

"Sure, that works for me," Donna said.

"Sounds good. Where to?" Betty asked.

"Actually —" Dan began but stopped short. A pickup truck drove away from the estate's greenhouse, with Lang's familiar figure at the wheel. Dan had a sudden urge to know a little more about the so-called gardener. "How about the coffee shop at the

Colony Hotel? It's got old-world charm and... uh, the best club sandwiches in Beaumont."

"Club sandwiches?" Donna raised an eyebrow with a playful smirk. "Not a burger? Since when have you started putting on the Ritz?"

"Since now," Dan said with a grin. He made a broad gesture toward the mansion. "It's because of the high-class company I keep."

Donna and Betty exchanged glances, rolling their eyes in unison. The group strolled towards the white convertible Betty had borrowed from her family. Just as they reached it, the Cadillac pulled up to the front door. Romero emerged from the driver's seat, his eyes immediately landing on Dan. The chauffeur gave him a calm, emotionless gaze, giving no indication of what had happened between them last night.

"Who is that dreamboat?" Donna breathed out.

"Chauffeur," Dan answered as he ushered her into Betty's car. "Married, has a raft of kids, a house with a white picket fence, dog, canary... the whole bit."

They arrived at the Colony Hotel a short time later, and Dan spotted Lang's truck tucked away in the parking lot. Once an opulent establishment, it had seen better days, but still maintained a certain charm and allure. The richly decorated lobby was now adorned with worn carpets and furniture, a marked difference from the polished luxury it must have once displayed.

Dan led the way into the hotel's coffee shop. The group took a booth near the back, with Dan taking a seat with a clear view of the lobby. After they told the waitress what they wanted, Betty pulled out a notepad.

"Okay, first, some background you'll need." Betty opened to a page. "Executive Order 6102, issued by President Roosevelt in 1933, required all persons in the United States to turn over before May 1, 1933, all gold coin, gold bullion, and gold certificates to a Federal bank in exchange for..." she checked her notes "... $20.67 per troy ounce."

"So if anyone stashed gold instead of turning it in, they'd be in huge trouble with the government," Dan said.

"You bet." Betty tapped her finger against the notepad. "Fines of up to $10,000, or up to ten years in prison, or both."

"So now we come to Mr. Maitland. An article appeared in the newspaper in November 1939, reporting he didn't show up for a court date." Donna leaned forward as she lowered her voice. "He was about to be indicted for violations of federal law, conspiracy, and fraud."

"For not turning in his gold?" Dan asked. He stopped as the waitress brought their club sandwiches. Dan cocked an eyebrow at the petite triangles of toast, bacon, lettuce, and tomato. At least the side order of fries would fill him up a little.

"Exactly," Donna said as she picked up her sandwich. "Maitland apparently skedaddled out of the country instead of standing trial, although his attorney didn't know for sure. Or didn't say for the record, at least. The article reported a rumor that a witness spotted Maitland boarding a plane, making tracks for South America."

"The same time Maitland 'went abroad', according to Andrew. Sounded like he screamed 'guilty'." Dan popped a fry into his mouth. "How did the Feds find out the violations?"

"Anonymous tip to the Treasury Department, according to the news," Donna said. "Nothing more about the case after that. I suppose there still is a warrant out for him. The next mention in the papers of the Belmont Foundry came in 1943. It was a profile of Tony Dietz, who took over the business after Maitland fled."

"From hired hand to owner. Not bad." Dan nodded as he took a bite of his sandwich.

"Why all the interest in the Maitlands?" Donna's gaze locked with Dan's. "You and Paul aren't involved in discovering another stash of embezzled money again, are you? Like last summer?"

"Or you two haven't stumbled on another protection racket, have you?" Betty asked.

Dan grinned. "No, and no. This is more like 'unofficial assistance to Detective Barton' level stuff. About the disappearance of Andrew Maitland," he said. "But it may not be so mysterious. Mrs. Maitland said he took a trip to California without telling her first."

Donna crossed her arms. "Which you don't believe."

"Well, it's not that... I mean, you know, it's just... well, Mrs. Maitland told me that he did, but..." Dan fumbled.

Donna and Betty looked at each other. "He doesn't believe it," they said as one.

Dan agreed with a nod. "Okay, I don't. Something about this doesn't sit well with me. It's like sometimes when I'm looking at my art — a painting or photograph — and I can sense something about it isn't quite right… composition, color, light. It's hard to pinpoint at first, but I know there's something off somewhere."

"The Case twins—always neck-deep in another caper," said Betty. "If you two were any more magnetic to trouble, you'd need your own radio series."

"Don't forget to throw in some books, too," Donna said with a laugh.

Dan, Donna, and Betty finished eating, then shuffled into the lobby. Donna glanced at Dan. "Okay, why did we come here again? The food was fine but…"

"Shh." Dan cut her off mid-sentence as he spotted Albert Lang emerging from the elevator. With a subtle grasp of the girls' elbows, Dan guided Donna and Betty toward the newsstand, feigning interest in a *Modern Screen* magazine featuring the latest teen heartthrob on the cover.

"Since when have you been interested in Frank Sinatra?" Donna asked.

"I'm trying to figure out why you girls scream over a skinny guy like him," he whispered, without looking up from the glossy pages. "Look busy."

Donna and Betty picked out a *Photoplay* and *Silver Screen*. Out of the corner of his eye, Dan saw Lang slap his room key onto the registration desk before heading towards the exit. The clerk, engrossed in a phone call, paid no attention to the abandoned key.

"Betty, Donna, I need a distraction. Keep the clerk occupied at the far end of the counter," Dan said in a quiet voice, putting the magazine back and nudging them toward the front desk's direction. "Think you can handle that?"

"Watch and learn, handsome," Donna said with a wink, striding to the front counter with Betty at her side. She waited until the desk clerk hung up. "Excuse me, sir. We're lost. Can you give us directions to Farmingville?"

"There's no such place around here, miss," the clerk patiently answered. "There is a Farm—"

"Not Farmingville," Betty piped up, annoyed. "It's Farmington... *ton*."

"Miss, there's also no—" the clerk attempted.

"Are you sure?" Donna fired back at Betty. "I distinctly remember being told Farming*ville*. Or maybe it was Farming Center."

The girls continued to argue, ignoring the flustered room clerk's attempts to intervene. As Dan strolled past the reception desk, he swiped Lang's key as if performing a magic trick. Without missing a beat, he made his way to the elevator and pressed the up arrow. He glanced at the number 217 engraved on the key tag, pushing the "2" button when he stepped into the cab.

Once arriving at the floor, he walked down the corridor with its garish floral-patterned carpet until he reached a door adorned with a shiny brass plaque displaying 217. Acting as though he was a hotel guest, he unlocked the door and entered. Stepping inside Lang's room, Dan pocketed the key.

He stood in a short hallway, with the closet on one side and the bathroom door on the other. He began a careful search, making sure not to disturb anything. A check of the closet revealed nothing but a gardener's work clothes, soiled and smelling faintly of earth and sweat. The bathroom didn't turn up anything unusual.

Next, he turned his attention to the desk. Easing out the drawer, he spotted an envelope. Gently lifting it by the open flat, he gave a low whistle when he saw the contents. Five crisp $20 bills nestled inside. Not bad for a man who prunes roses and trims hedges, Dan thought.

As he tucked the envelope back into its hiding place, the murmur of voices and footsteps in the corridor reached his ears. Dan's pulse quickened.

"It's not a bother, sir. Guests forget their keys inside all the time," a voice said. "The doors lock automatically when they shut."

Dan froze. The footsteps stopped outside room 217. A metallic rattle announced a key inserted into the lock.

Chapter Eight

Dan's fingers closed around the cool metal of the key. He pulled it out of his pocket and sent it skittering across the patterned carpet to rest by the door with an artful flick of his wrist, born of fear.

Dropping on his back, with no grace whatsoever, he wriggled under the double bed. The dust bunnies keeping him company gave testimony to the hotel's less than thorough room cleaning. After carefully pushing the mattress skirt back into place, he laid flat. He held his breath and tried to merge with the floor. It was like playing hide-and-seek with stakes higher than just his pride on the line.

The door creaked open and footsteps entered the room.

"Why see there, Mr. Lang, sir," a voice chirped with a note of eagerness only found in those working for tips. It must be a bellhop. "It looks like you've dropped your key here."

Lang's reply was a low grunt that rumbled through the floorboards. "I thought I left it at the front desk."

"Could be, sir, could be," the bellhop said with a chuckle. "But unless it sprouted legs and wandered back, there it is. Don't worry. Our guests do that all the time."

"Must've slipped my mind," Lang conceded, his voice gruff. A light, metallic tinkle sounded as the key was picked up. It was followed by the crinkling of some bills. "Here. For your trouble."

"Thank you, sir," the bellhop said.

Score one for the bellman, Dan thought. He scooted out, closing the door behind him with a soft click. Dan let out his breath quietly.

Lang sat on the bed, its springs creaking. "I could have sworn I put this on the front desk," he mumbled to himself.

The cramped region beneath the bed grew suffocating to Dan, crushing down on him. How much longer would the gardener linger? Would Dan be trapped here until Lang fell asleep that night? The thought of spending hours in this confined space made his heart race. Suddenly, he needed to pee.

Lang got up. Footsteps crossed to the desk, and the drawer slid open. Paper rustled.

A random speck of dust danced its way into Dan's nostril, tickling the sensitive lining with the finesse of a feather duster wielded by a clumsy maid.

"Ah — Don't you dare," Dan silently pleaded with his own nose, squeezing his eyes closed and screwing up his face as the urge to sneeze swelled within him like an expanding balloon. He pinched his nostrils, fighting the reflex with all the might his seventeen-year-old sinuses could muster.

Agonizing seconds later, the desk drawer closed again. With deliberate movements, Lang slipped out, leaving the room.

Dan's defenses held firm until a few moments after the door clicked shut behind Lang. That's when his nose betrayed him, releasing the pent-up sneeze with the force of an atomic bomb.

"Achoo!"

The sound echoed like a trumpet blast at midnight. Dan's head met the bottom slats of the bed with a thud that would've made any cartoon character have tweeting birds and stars drawn circling his head.

"Ow," he muttered, rubbing the sore spot as he slid out from his dusty refuge. He climbed to his feet and approached the desk. Time to see what Lang was up to.

Dan opened the drawer and peeked into the envelope. It was now deflated by one less picture of President Jackson. Closing the drawer, he scanned the room with the scrutiny of a seasoned sleuth. Which, by now, he considered himself one.

The room was barren, devoid of any personal touch. No photos, no knickknacks, not even a stray sock. If Lang lived here, as he claimed, why would the grumpy gardener not have added some homey touches, like a book by the bed or a portable radio? It appeared as impersonal as what it was: a temporary place to sleep.

So maybe Lang didn't live here, Dan pondered. He has another house but is using the hotel as a blind. Why go to the expense? Especially with a free cottage available on the mansion grounds?

Dan cast a last glance around the sterile room when his artist's eye latched onto a last-minute detail. On the notepad by the telephone, a series of indents caught the light slanting through the window. Something had been written on the sheet just above. He picked up the pencil next to it and shaded the paper. He squinted, angling the pad to catch the sunlight just right. The impression of a phone number emerged as if by magic.

"KL5-2000. Gotcha," he said in triumph. He tore off the page before replacing the notepad in the exact location he found it. With the stealth of a cat burglar, he pressed his ear against the room door, hearing nothing but the sound of his own heightened pulse. Convinced the coast was clear, Dan slipped out into the hall and walked confidently as though he were a guest.

He used the stairs, bypassing the elevator in case Lang potentially made another surprise return visit. Striding through the lobby and out the hotel's revolving door, Dan stopped. The familiar voices of Donna and Betty greeted him, calling his name. They were seated in the convertible. Dan jogged up.

"Hey, you two!" Dan said, skidding to a stop. "Thanks! You two were great!"

"What was that all about?" Betty challenged. "We've become accomplices in what crazy scheme of yours?"

"And why come to this hotel?" Donna demanded. "Fess up there."

Dan held up both hands to deflect the barrage. "Okay, okay, I'll spill. Albert Lang is supposed to live here, but I'm thinking he doesn't."

Betty and Donna looked at each other, then back at Dan, and shrugged.

"He's the gardener out at the Maitland place. Well, that's what he claims to be." Dan explained how Paul believed Lang was a phony, and how Dan saw him drive away from the estate earlier. "I spotted him coming out of the elevator, put his key on the front desk so—"

Donna broke in. "You had us distract the clerk, so you could steal the key to have a little look-see around the phony gardener's room."

"Borrowed... borrowed the key," Dan corrected. "Lang got it back."

"All right, handsome, what did you find? The crown jewels?" Donna asked.

"No, a telephone number!" Dan pulled out the shaded piece of paper in triumph.

Neither Betty nor Donna appeared impressed.

Dan didn't care. He raced on as he examined the note. "Do either of you know if the KL exchange is local?"

"I never heard of it." Donna looked at Betty, who shook her head. "What's the deal?"

"This number I found on the pad—KL5-2000," Dan said. "I'm curious who would be on the other end. That may be the actual clue."

"Of course, that could have been written by the room's previous guest, and has nothing to do with that guy," Betty pointed out.

Dan hadn't considered that. "Ah..."

"Or, it could just be for a pizza parlor," Donna shrugged.

"Ah..."

Donna stepped in to save him. "Well, let's get to a phone booth and find out before flies buzz into your open mouth." Dan nodded in agreement as he vaulted into the back seat. "What are you going to say if somebody answers? 'I found your number on a pad in the hotel room I broke into'?"

Dan hadn't really thought of that, either. He thought for a moment. "Say 'sorry, wrong number', I guess."

Donna tapped her temple and leaned toward Betty. She nodded to Dan. "Handsome *and* smart, this one is."

"But first I want to know the location of the KL telephone exchange," Dan said.

They drove to the nearest drugstore, a bustling hub of activity that dwarfed Mr. Allen's small store in Farmingford where Dan worked. The bright fluorescent lights flickered overhead. The familiar scent of disinfectant and bubblegum wafted through the air, creating a strange but not unpleasant combination. Shelves upon shelves of products lined the aisles, each one promising a quick fix for any ailment or problem. Or boxes of candy and aftershave lotion for that last-minute forgotten gift.

As he entered the phone booth, Dan couldn't help but notice the spacious lunch counter nearby. He briefly dreamed about how much more in tips he could make working here. Closing the balky, folding door behind him, Dan picked up the receiver. He inserted a coin into the slot and dialed the operator.

A crisp, professional voice came over the wire. "Operator."

"Operator, can you tell me where the KL exchange is located?" Dan asked.

"One moment, sir." The operator clicked off. Dan exchanged hopeful glances with Donna and Betty through the glass in the doors.

The operator returned. "The KL exchange is Klamath. Its location is Washington, DC." The operator's voice crackled through the line.

"Could you connect me with Long Distance, please?" Dan asked. He cracked open the door and held out his hand. "Long distance."

"Need change?" Donna dug through her purse like a miner panning for gold. Betty did as well.

"Long Distance," a second operator pronounced.

"I'd like to make a Station-to-station call to Klamath 5-2000," Dan said as the girls dropped coins into his palm. He smiled a thanks.

"Klamath 5-2000. Fifty cents for three minutes." The operator somehow added a syllable to "three."

Dan fed the hungry slot, and the phone clanged as it ingested its meal. The silence gave way to a ringing that seemed to sound as far away as Washington, DC, was. Ring after ring, Dan's hope waned, and the number remained unanswered.

The operator came back on the line. "Your party is not answering."

Dan thanked the operator and placed the receiver back on the hook. The change clattered back into the coin return. He scooped it out and returned the money to Donna. "Turns out our mystery guest wasn't home. Maybe was out taking a drive."

"It could be it's an office and not open today. It's Sunday, after all," Donna said.

"Right," Dan conceded. "Betty, can you get Paul to call Klamath 5-2000 tomorrow? It may be nothing, but I still want to know whose number it is. Have him let me know."

"Will do," she said with a nod.

Dan sighed. He had little to show for the afternoon's work of poking around. So much for being a seasoned sleuth. "Thanks for coming to lunch with me, girls, and the information on Maitland."

"Will it be of any help?" Donna asked.

"I don't know." Dan shrugged and checked his watch. "I should get back now. But while I'm here, I want to buy a flashlight."

"Then we shall return the king to his castle," Betty said in a grand tone.

Dan gave a rueful smile. "Right now, I feel more like the court jester."

The Cadillac, with its trunk open, stood at the front door of the Maitland Mansion as Betty's white convertible pulled up. She braked to a stop.

"Somebody going somewhere?" Donna asked.

"Not that I know of," Dan answered as he climbed out.

"Maybe it's not going but coming. It could be Andrew has come home," Betty said.

"Like Lassie?" Dan was doubtful as he slammed the door shut and whispered. "Still have Paul check out that number."

Betty and Donna drove off with a wave. Dan stepped over the threshold into the grand foyer, almost stumbling over a suitcase sitting on the stone floor. Dan checked the luggage tag: Mrs. Margaret Maitland. So it wasn't bags from Andrew's home-coming.

Dan ran upstairs to his room, tossing the flashlight and bat-teries on the bed. He had gone back downstairs and reached the entry when he heard his name.

"Daniel, dear boy!" Mrs. Maitland's voice, smooth as silk and twice as rich, enveloped him before she appeared from around the corner, her silver hair catching the light like a beacon. "I'm glad I can tell you in person, instead of leaving a note. Oh, I have the most thrilling news!"

"Really?" Dan said.

"Indeed! My dearest friend, who lives in New York City, just called me to say The Met is performing 'La Boheme.' It is my absolute favorite." She closed her eyes and lifted her chin, launching into song with the gusto of a slightly off-key opera diva. "Che gelida manina, se la lasci riscaldar..." She accompa-nied her singing with a few dance steps.

"Uh, that's great, Mrs. Maitland," Dan said once her im-promptu recital ended. "So, when are you off to New York?"

"Today! Right now! As soon as Maribelle — that's my friend — hung up, I reserved a Pullman on the evening train out of Chicago." She beamed at him. "I shall bask in Puccini's genius, then Maribelle and I will browse the shops along Fifth Avenue. I will make a week of it and return next Monday."

"Sounds... enchanting. I hope you have a good time," Dan said. "I'll just call Paul to pick me up then—"

"Nonsense!" Mrs. Maitland declared with a flippant wave of her hand. "You simply must remain. You need to finish your painting."

"Well, I've made enough progress now that I can continue to work at my house — I mean, in my studio," Dan said.

"Daniel," Mrs. Maitland said, her tone leaving no room for argument, "I commissioned you to do a plein aire painting. I expect a plein aire painting."

Don't need to send me a telegram, Dan thought. "Of course. I'll stay and keep working on it."

"Excellent. Oh, and Mrs. Danner is taking the opportunity to visit her sister while I'm out of town. She's already left," Mrs. Maitland went on. "Can you cook?"

"Er, yes, but—" Dan started.

"Perfect! Mrs. Danner has stocked the larder. At least you shan't be a starving artist!" She trilled a laugh. "Romero will take care of locking up the house at night, so you needn't worry about that." Turning to the door, she called, "Romero, is the car ready?"

The chauffeur, as brooding as a storm cloud, materialized in the doorway.

"Yes, ma'am," Romero intoned, his icy stare piercing Dan.

Mrs. Maitland gestured to the driver. "See? You really won't be alone. Although Lang is off starting tomorrow for the next few days, Romero will be here."

That was about as comforting to Dan as bunking with Jack the Ripper. "Can my brother come over, too?" he asked.

"Of course, Daniel! The more, the merrier! Just pick one of the rooms across from yours!" Mrs. Maitland wagged an admonishing finger between Dan and Romero. "Just no wild parties, you two!"

Dan hadn't even attended a wild party, much less know how to throw one. He managed a chuckle. Romero's expression never changed. "I won't. I promise."

Mrs. Maitland checked her watch. "Oh! We must fly to catch the train!" She stopped and giggled. "'Fly to catch the train!' Just listen to me! Oh, how silly! That's what the thought of basking in Puccini's genius does to me!" She fluttered toward the open door, Romero in tow with her suitcase.

As the front door slammed shut behind them, its echo resounding through the foyer, Dan couldn't shake the feeling that he'd just been sealed inside a tomb. When the Cadillac's motor faded in the distance, he stepped outside.

Brutus and Max ran up to him. Dan scratched their heads, then his mind darted back to Lang. He decided to check the lodging the gardener wouldn't use. Maybe there was a good reason. After all, the place could be rundown or something. Accompanied by the dogs, he set off.

The gardener's cottage and greenhouse stood nestled next to the hedge maze. Dan's gaze was immediately drawn to the shining glass walls and roof of the hothouse. He pushed open the door and was met with a rush of warm, humid air as he stepped inside. Tall wooden tables lining the sides, most likely intended for plants. However, empty pots were all they held currently.

In fact, the entire hothouse seemed to be unused, except for a few bags of garden soil in one corner that appeared as if they had been there for quite some time. A pile of well-used gardening tools clustered nearby.

The cottage sat next to the greenhouse. While the mansion resembled a grand castle, the tiny house exuded the charm of a small village home, built in a picturesque half-timbered Tudor style with charming accents. The rugged fieldstone chimney jutted out proudly from the roofline. It was as if the building had been plucked straight out of a fairytale, transporting visitors to a simpler time and place.

Dan approached the cottage, its windows sealed shut with sturdy wooden shutters. He tried to peek inside, but the tight slats blocked his view. Frustrated, he made his way to the front door and tested the handle. Unsurprisingly, it was locked.

As he turned to leave, a faint sound — a thud — from inside caught Dan's attention. He checked on Max and Brutus. The dogs were on high alert, their ears perked up and heads tilted towards the small building.

Dan walked back to the door and pressed his ear next to it, listening for any signs of movement or sound from the cottage. He rattled the knob. After a moment of silence, he started away again.

But then, a sharp scratching echoed from above as a squirrel scurried down the tree with a branch that extended over the roof. The dogs immediately began barking and chasing after the critter, their paws pounding against the ground as they raced off toward their target.

Dan laughed. There was the source of the noise. He turned and jumped. Lang stood behind him.

"What are you doing here, kid?" the gardener growled.

"I was taking Max and Brutus out for a walk. They saw a squirrel and took off." Dan pointed in the direction the Max and Brutus disappeared.

"Why here? Why around this cottage?" Lang took a threatening step closer.

"Well, Mrs. Danner told me about this place, and when you drove off. I thought you had left for the day, so —"

Lang stabbed an accusing finger at Dan. "You're snoopin' for that old society biddy, aren't you? Checking out if I'm doing my work or not, is that it?"

"No, I'm not," Dan protested.

"Well, you tell those high and mighty dames up in the castle that I went to town to buy some garden soil. I just got back and dumped the bags in there." Lang jerked his thumb toward the greenhouse. "You just tell them that."

Max and Brutus bounded back to Dan's side, and he was glad for their company. He didn't know what to say to Lang, but he knew he wanted to get away from the gardener as soon as possible. Dan gave the dogs a pat on their heads before saying, "Let's get out of here, boys."

Dan started to go, but Lang grabbed his arm. He leaned in and spoke intensely. "Listen to me, sonny. Be careful up there in that grand house. Beware of them... all of them. Like that housekeep-er..."

"Mrs. Danner?"

"Yeah, that's what she calls herself. Now. She ain't what she seems. Take my word for it. Watch out for her... and especially your back around her. And that Romero... never trust foreigners." He went on in a harsh whisper, "You just look alive unless you want to end up like Andrew."

"He's in California."

Lang's laugh was short and sharp, sounding like a bark. "Is he? That's what they want you to believe, sonny boy."

Dan was losing his fear of Lang and grew just plain annoyed. He couldn't hide the sarcasm. "Are you suggesting Mrs. Danner or Romero planted Andrew under one of your prize flower beds instead?"

"Wise guy," the gardener released his grip. With one final scowl at Dan, he strode toward the hedges and disappeared from sight.

Dan looked down at Max and Brutus. "Are you two the only ones I can trust around here?" He guessed the outburst was the reason Lang didn't stay on the property. Who would want to live around him?

The trio headed back to the mansion. When they passed the greenhouse, Dan peeked inside. Only the three bags of garden soil he'd seen before were there. Lang hadn't added a thing.

The late afternoon shadows crept in, swallowing the grandiose mansion as Dan stepped into the foyer. The gothic architecture that had impressed him earlier now turned foreboding and ominous, especially with no one else there. Hungry, he walked to the kitchen, taking care to memorize every light switch on the way so he wouldn't be caught in the dark like the other night.

He assembled a huge sandwich with thick slabs of meat and cheese. After pouring himself a tall glass of milk, he carried his food into the dining room and ate under the unblinking gaze of the mounted animals on the walls. After finishing his meal, he washed his dishes and rummaged through cabinets until his fingers closed around a sleeve of chocolate chip cookies. With a contented smile, he went into the living room, wondering what would be on TV tonight.

The final bar of the "Star-Spangled Banner" faded hours later, signaling the end of the television station's broadcast day. Dan stood up and stretched. He turned off the set and stared at the now dark screen, almost expecting to see the mysterious figure once again. But it never appeared, and Dan let out a relieved sigh before heading upstairs.

Max and Brutus had got there first. They were already sprawled on the floor, the door slightly ajar from when they barged in. Dan couldn't suppress his grin at the scene, but it quickly disappeared as he shut the door behind him.

A knife pinned a note to the back of the door.

Chapter Nine

Dan stood stunned for a moment, his gaze fixed on the note. He grabbed the paper and yanked the blade from the wood. Examining the knife closer, he seemed as if it came from the kitchen — one of Mrs. Danner's. He turned to the dogs.

"Is this handiwork yours?" he asked them, holding the knife and the note up. Max yawned.

Putting the knife on the bedside table, he read the type-written message. "If you want to uncover the truth, begin in Andrew's bedroom. Be observant of even the smallest details that others may miss. But be careful — once you enter this room, there's no going back."

He sat on the bed, lost in thought for a moment. The last note had given him a crucial clue... perhaps there was such a thing as fate, after all. He reached for the flashlight he had just bought and loaded the batteries. If he was going to sneak into someone else's bedroom at midnight and poke around, he might as well look the part. Tucking the paper into his hip pocket, he headed out of his room.

The house was now eerily quiet, empty, as still as death. He couldn't shake off the feeling of being an intruder in a stranger's home. Technically, he was, Dan told himself, but he was not a burglar... he was an invited guest. That made searching a room not his in a house not his a little less... less... He finally settled on the term "unethical."

His eyes darted around, looking for any signs of movement. Nothing. Nor was there any sound. Where was Romero? How long could dropping Mrs. Maitland off at the train station take? It had been a while since the chauffeur left and Dan didn't want to take any chances being found by him rummaging through Andrew's possessions. Romero already made it plain he could make things "unpleasant" for Dan. It could be more so with no witnesses in the area.

Taking slow, cautious steps, he went to Andrew's room. He paused before he gripped the knob and pushed the door open. Leaving the lamp off, he switched on his flashlight and swept the beam around the tidy room. He went in, shutting the door behind him softly. Start with the obvious, he decided.

Dan walked up to the closet and checked inside. Like other old houses he'd seen, the closet was surprisingly small, but packed with a neat collection of expensive clothing, almost like at a department store. There were some gaps where items had been taken out, as one would expect if someone were preparing for a trip. Nothing to see here. He was about to close the door when he remembered the note: "Be observant of even the smallest details".

On closer inspection, something caught his eye. He shone his flashlight on the empty spots where the clothes used to hang and noticed not only were the garments missing, but the hangers were gone as well. It struck him as odd. Most people would leave the hangers when putting clothes in a suitcase. It seemed like whoever took these items was trying to create the illusion of packing for a trip, but was in a hurry. They snatched clothing with everything still attached. That probably meant Andrew's supposed journey to California was a fabrication all along.

Continuing his search, Dan dropped to his knees and peered under the bed, finding nothing but shadows and dust. Checking behind the headboard yielded no secrets, either. He rifled through the dresser next, noting the jumbled voids where underwear and socks should have been. It was as if someone had clawed them out without looking, unconcerned with what was taken and what was left.

He opened the desk, shuffling through mundane items until an envelope with a travel agency logo caught his eye. Inside was an itinerary for travel to Argentina—not to California, and dated for February of this year.

Dan's thoughts raced: was this a hidden journey? Was that where Andrew got his tan since the winter and summer seasons were reversed between the hemispheres? Donna informed him Mr. Maitland was suspected of fleeing to South America to avoid trial. Did Andrew take this trip to follow the sun down south, instead of a vacation in Palm Springs, like he said to his mother? Or was the visit to his father? Was it a route he regularly took? And if not, why start now?

He returned the envelope and pulled out a file folder. On the tab, written in a strong hand, was "Tony Dietz." Flipping it open, he saw three newspaper clippings. One was the story about Mr. Maitland not appearing in court. The other two were about Dietz... how we took over the company and the profile about him. The same ones Donna had referred to, Dan supposed. The inside surfaces of the folder were filled with notes, but they were single words that meant nothing to Dan. Many of the words were circled, with arrows pointing to other words or question marks. Andrew must have been using the folder as a scratch pad as he thought through something.

After staring at the scribbles for a few minutes, Dan shook his head. He couldn't make heads or tails of them. He placed the folder back inside the desk drawer.

Dan scanned the rest of the room. His eyes landed on a table by the window, which held a collection of books. Among them were leather-bound works by Edgar Allan Poe and H.P. Lovecraft, as well as classic horror novels like *Dracula*, *Frankenstein*, and *Dr. Jekyll and Mr. Hyde*. Next to these standouts were contemporary paperback crime thrillers such as *The Lady in the Lake*, *Kiss Me Deadly*, and *Nightmare Alley*. Also in the stack were pulp magazines with lurid covers.

Andrew's taste for macabre obviously went beyond just reading news stories about murder or having "grand fun" at Halloween parties held at the mansion.

Dan picked up each book, flipping through the pages. When he reached Poe's "The Pit and the Pendulum", a couple of pieces of folded paper fell out. He walked to his desk and opened them, smoothing out the creases. With his flashlight in hand, he examined it: a photostat of a ledger page. A typed note accompanied it. "This is only a sample. The price will go up. Decide", it read.

That read like a blackmail demand. Was Andrew being blackmailed, and when he refused to pay, kidnapped? Dan straightened up when he considered another idea. Or was Andrew the blackmailer? His victim didn't fork out, but instead took revenge by doing away with Andrew?

A sudden metallic rattle snapped Dan out of his thoughts. He pivoted on his heels, shining his flashlight on the doorknob. It was jiggling and turning as if someone was attempting to enter the room from the hallway. Dan hesitated, considering whether he should either hide in the closet or try to come up with an excuse for whoever was on the other side... especially if it happened to be Romero.

The knob stopped moving. Gathering his courage, Dan strode to the door and flung it open with a forceful swing. The only thing waiting for him in the hall was silence.

Dan went back to his room and sat on the bed, examining the ledger page, trying to figure out if the numbers gave any clue. He didn't know, but he had to get this stuff to Detective Barton.

A muffled cry and thud from downstairs upset his thoughts. Dan's pulse quickened as he tossed the papers aside and bounded down the stairs.

The hallway was dark. Dan remembered where the switch was and flipped on the lights. At the far end of the corridor lay Romero, sprawled on the stone floor like a broken puppet. Dan rushed up to him.

"Romero! Are you alright?" Dan knelt beside him.

"Damn," grumbled Romero, gingerly touching the bleeding cut on his forehead. "Yes, I'm fine."

Dan helped the chauffeur to his feet. "What happened?"

There was a moment's hesitation. "I was locking up the house, and I tripped, that's all." Romero's voice was strained, but emphatic.

Dan looked around the hallway. It was free of any obstruction that could cause a fall. "Tripped over what?"

"I tripped, fell, and bumped my head. That is all that happened," Romero stressed as his final answer.

"Okay, okay. You tripped and went down. Message received," Dan said. "Do you need any help to take care of the cut?"

The cold, professional demeanor returned. "No, sir. I can manage. Thank you, sir." For a moment, it seemed as if Romero wanted to say something else, but instead, he turned away.

Dan watched the chauffeur shuffle back into the kitchen. Could Romero have been the one outside the door of Andrew's room, then, for some reason, bolted and fell as he fled? Before he could pursue his thoughts any further, the agitated barks of Max and Brutus sliced through his confusion.

"Now what?" Dan groused as he ran back upstairs.

The dogs were in the hall, barking and scratching at the bedroom door, desperate to get inside. Dan stopped. He didn't close it on his way out. No time to consider that now. He pushed past Great Danes and reached for the knob. Just as he did, the door opened and the cloaked figure emerged. At last, Dan saw its face.

A skull peered back at him from under the cowl, the face of somebody long dead, glowing with an eerie green hue all its own. Dan couldn't suppress his gasp as he instinctively took a step back from the frightening sight.

With a sudden shove, the monk sent Dan tumbling backward. He struggled to regain his balance but fell to the floor as the thing glided down the hallway. Max and Brutus bounded over to Dan.

"No, no! Not me!" Dan shouted to the dogs, pointing to the monk as it disappeared around the far corner of the hall. "It! It!"

Max and Brutus chased after the figure while Dan got to his feet and followed. Turning sharply, feet slipping on the wooden floorboards, the pursuers ended up in a short hall. Two doors stood on one side and a lone door on the opposite wall. At the end was a window. Max and Brutus circled the area, sniffing, trying to track down the elusive — and now vanished — monk.

"Ah, you can't do that to me again," Dan whined. He added after a pause, "Can you?"

Dan checked the first door to his left. It turned out to be a stuffed linen closet. The next door was locked, and the window was latched from the inside. He peered through the glass. Even if it was unlatched, there was a two-story drop to the ground.

With a deep breath, Dan gingerly pushed open the third door, using only his fingertips. The hinges creaked, and he froze, listening for any sounds of movement from inside. Slipping his hand through the crack, his fingers grasped the light switch, and he turned it on. He waited a few more moments before fully opening the door and stepping in.

The room was small, with a single bed against one wall and a dresser on the other side. A faint scent of furniture wax lingered in the air. A quick search of the room uncovered no one lurking in, under, or behind anything. The window was also locked from the inside. The mysterious monk had successfully executed another disappearing act.

Back in his own room, Dan's gaze swept the bed. The papers he'd found were gone.

Dan sank on the bed and groaned. "Of course they are."

Max and Brutus raced back into the room, sitting at Dan's feet and resting their heads on his knees. As he petted them, Dan went through everything that had happened in his mind.

The only other person in the house was Romero. He couldn't have beaten Dan upstairs without passing him on the staircase. So he could be ruled out as the mysterious figure in the cloak, who must have also taken the papers. That meant someone else was in the house, perhaps slugged Romero, then moved throughout the mansion while Dan was busy downstairs.

At least he had one answer. The mystery monk was a human, not a spook. That shove proved it.

But why were the notes being left in the first place? They were designed to direct Dan to various clues, but how come? And by whom? Was this whole thing some kind of gigantic game?

Dan wished his brother was here so he could talk things over with him. He looked down at the dogs. "Detectives in the books I read always have the answers. All I've got are questions. You guys got any ideas?"

***

Paul sat in Detective Barton's office on Monday morning, surrounded by sparse furnishings. He couldn't help but think that there must be a store somewhere called "The Big Ugly Steel Office Furniture Company." The chair he sat on was hard and uncomfortable, made of metal with a thin seat pad covered in an unidentifiable green plastic-vinyl material that defied description. His knees brushed against the cold and utilitarian desk, which had a metal top that was supposed to look like wood but failed miserably. Behind the desk was a swivel armchair with the same ugly green material covering the seat and armrests. A short bookcase filled with official-looking books stood against one wall.

The room was stark, functional, and devoid of warmth—much like the furniture. Paul's eyes roamed around the dull, lifeless walls of the office. A framed, black-and-white photograph caught his attention, showcasing a powerful destroyer churning through ocean waves. Probably the ship Barton served on during the war. Next to it was a more personal snapshot, revealing Barton surrounded by his fellow sailors, their bond evident in their relaxed stances and shared laughter.

But what struck Paul more was what was missing — there were no photos of anyone who could be a wife, fiancée, or girlfriend. As Barton entered the room, file in hand, Paul noticed the absence of a wedding ring on the detective's left hand. Paul recalled how friendly Barton and his mother appeared that afternoon at his house. Now, for some reason, the memory made him uncomfortable. Maybe even resentful.

"The car you saw go into the river," Barton began, reading the paper in the file as he walked toward his chair, "was reported stolen out of Chicago three weeks ago. Dead end there, I'm afraid." He continued reading, then paused and glanced at Paul with respect. "Diving in the water to save the driver. Took guts." He sat at his desk and closed the folder. "Seems like courage is a family trait."

"Guess it might be," Paul admitted with a shrug.

"Your mother, Alice... Mrs. Case," Barton went on, a smile playing on his lips and the admiration in his voice unmistakable, "strikes me as formidable and strong. Quite a remarkable woman."

You don't know the half of it, Paul thought. Last summer, the brothers discovered a shocking bit of history. When teens, their parents had been involved in gangster Lorenzo Rizzo's bootlegging business in Chicago during Prohibition. Their mother insisted neither of them was caught up in any "rough stuff". However, when their father barely escaped a fatal ambush on Rizzo's gang, Dan and Paul's parents decided to leave everything behind and start fresh. They eloped and settled down in Farmingford to start a family.

"So was my dad." Paul's voice was proud... and defensive.

"I'm sure he was," Barton agreed.

The two of them sat in silence for a moment, the only sounds in the room coming from the constant ringing of phones, closing doors, and footsteps echoing in the hallway.

"I'm glad you came in here this morning, Paul." Barton pulled another folder out from his desk. "While I was out of town, Mrs. Maitland canceled the missing person report. Closed the case. She said Andrew went to California and didn't tell her ahead of time. So you can tell Dan to stand down."

"And you believe her?"

Barton tapped the file. "She's his mother, Paul. If she says he went to California, he went to California. We have little reason to contest it without evidence to the contrary. And Andrew is not a minor."

Paul leaned forward. "Dan's notes. What about Dan's notes I told you about? I read them. One said for Dan to go look in some kind of maze for a clue. When he did, he found another one telling Andrew to meet somebody there to learn 'something of benefit'."

"Who sent the notes, Paul?"

Paul threw up his hands in frustration. "How do I know? They were anonymous! But they point to something more than just a simple trip out West is involved," he shot back, thrusting a finger in the air as if the physical act could summon the missing papers.

"And the ledger sheet I found. What about that? It was in the coat pocket of the driver from the car that crashed into the river!"

"How does the ledger connect to the Maitlands? What did it contain?" The detective leaned on his desk, folding his hands.

"Well... it... it had columns of numbers! And dates... and... and... other stuff!" Paul sputtered.

"Columns of numbers and other stuff," Barton repeated. He shook his head. "Paul, that's not—"

"It's got to be tied up with the notes." Paul's voice rose. "The car... it was heading to the Maitland place when it went into the drink."

"How do you know? Are you certain? There are more estates on that road." Barton's tone was steady, but there was a sharpness to it now, a detective's demand for facts.

"For a fact? No, I can't be," Paul admitted, his shoulders sinking a little. "But everything points to it being true."

Barton tilted back in his chair and spread his hands helplessly. "Without the actual documents, what you're telling me is hearsay, Paul. You know I can't act on that."

"What about Dan being watched? Somebody eavesdropping on him? What about that?" Paul demanded.

"Dan *thinks* he's being spied on." Barton's voice stayed in an even tone. "He's an artist. He has an active imagination."

Paul's face reddened, a flush of anger rising. He sat up straight in the chair. "So you don't believe me? Or Dan? Is that it? Do you think we made this all up?"

"Keep your shirt on now." Barton calmly raised a placating hand. "I didn't say that. I do believe you're concerned, and this isn't sitting right with you. But it's out of my hands. I cannot re-open Mrs. Maitland's missing persons case without solid evidence, suspicious circumstances, or potential foul play."

"Then what am I supposed to do?" Paul's voice rose, edged with irritation.

"Report the burglary to the Farmingford Sheriff's Department. It's the correct place to start," Barton said. "And thank Dan for all his work, but he's not needed any longer. I'll phone him when he gets back home and thank him myself."

And pick up on that nice, friendly conversation you were having with Mom too, I'll bet, Paul thought. "Thanks, Detective."

"Call me Steve," Barton said.

"Alright. Goodbye... Steve." Paul had to force himself to say the name.

As Paul left the office, he fumed at what the detective had said. After a minute or so, he calmed down. As he strode down the corridor, he had to admit to himself, Barton... Steve, that is... was correct. There was no hard evidence.

Okay. Case closed. It's kaput. Done. Over. Paul wondered if his brother would be disappointed at the turn of events.

Paul climbed into the jeep, casting a worried glance at the gray clouds bunching on the horizon. The weather report forecasted storms for the rest of the week. If he didn't mow lawns, he didn't get paid. As word of his reliability and top-notch work spread, he gained more customers, so he was determined to squeeze in as many jobs as he could before dark. It would make for a busy, exhausting day, but he didn't really care.

He enjoyed being outdoors, working with his hands, and the exercise of physical labor. And he hoped today it would also take his mind off his jumbled feelings about anything developing between Steve and Mom.

After driving home, he quickly changed into his work clothes, ready to set out once again, organizing the list of his clients mentally to maximize efficiency. On his way through the living room, he noticed the telephone and snapped his fingers. He promised Betty he would try the number Dan had given him through her. With the police closing the Maitland case, whatever Dan had hoped to learn from the call would be irrelevant. But the twins always upheld their promises to each other.

Paul detoured to the desk and placed the long-distance call to KA5-2000. He checked his watch as he waited.

A chipper voice answered. "United States Treasury Department."

Paul hadn't expected that. "Uh, who?"

"United States Treasury Department. Do you know your party's name or extension?"

"Uh, no. Sorry. I've reached the wrong number."

"That is all right. Good day, sir."

"Goodbye." Paul hung up the phone and stood still a moment, thinking.

Betty said Dan got the number from the gardener at the Maitland estate, although she wasn't exactly clear on how he got his hands on it. Why would a gardener — even a phony one Paul was sure Lang was — need to call the US Treasury Department in Washington, DC?

Chapter Ten

Dan groaned in exasperation. He squinted, trying to find the nuance that would define his work and capture the essence of the scene before him. Light and shadow danced across the mansion's walls, frustrating him because a detail he was working on would disappear into shadow as the sun slipped behind the moving clouds, only to pop back into brilliance a few seconds later.

A powerful gust buffeted the easel, sending a shiver through the frame. Dan steadied it with a firm hand, growling under his breath at the stormy weather.

He dipped his brush into the vibrant cerulean blue paint, taking care to mix it just right on his palette. He surveyed the ever-changing sky, and couldn't help but notice the ominous thunderclouds gathering in the distance. They were a bruise on the horizon, rolling closer with each passing moment.

The wind whipped at his clothes and hair as if warning him of the impending storm. Another blast threatened to overturn his easel, but Dan reacted quickly, dropping his brush and securing his work before any damage could be done. A movement drew his eyes away from his balancing act.

Romero slipped into the Cadillac, its engine starting with a low rumble. The chauffeur had mentioned earlier that the car needed to be taken to town to be serviced, implying that he couldn't take Dan anyplace that day. Not that Dan minded. The less time he spent around the glowering Romero, the better.

The green limousine still gleamed despite the cloudy sky as it drove down the driveway. Right on cue, Lang's truck emerged from behind the greenhouse and headed off in the same direction as the Cadillac. To Dan, that timing appeared a little too precise, too convenient.

The wind took another swipe at upsetting the easel. This is ridiculous, Dan thought as he made another grab for his work. With nobody else at the estate, Mrs. Maitland would never know if he worked inside or not. He packed up his supplies, carted them into the foyer, then scouted for a room to continue his work.

The tranquility of the morning room enveloped him as he crossed the threshold, an oasis of calm to the gathering storm outside. Soft light spilled through the French doors, casting dappled shadows on the Persian rug and antique furniture. This would be fine.

After carefully rolling up the carpet to avoid the slightest possibility of getting paint on it, he repositioned his easel by the French doors. Dan had just settled onto his stool when an unobtrusive presence of a portable typewriter case, nestled beside Mrs. Maitland's polished mahogany desk, snagged his attention.

A flicker of curiosity sparked in him as he retrieved the cryptic note from his pocket where he put it the night before. Unfolding the paper, he scrutinized the typeface. Each character was an actor in a mystery plot, but it was the letter "i" that took center stage, its slight height above the baseline of the other characters a potential clue.

An idea tugged at him as he glanced between the paper and the typewriter case several times. Maybe he could answer another of his many questions about this whole affair right now.

Going to the desk, he pulled out the typewriter and placed it on the blotter. The top drawer yielded a piece of paper, which he rolled into position with a soft clicking. Hunched over the machine, Dan began to hunt and peck, replicating the message left stabbed to his door, each keystroke punctuating the hush of the room like a tiny firecracker.

With the last letter hammered into place, Dan released a breath. He lifted the finished sheet from the roller, aligning it alongside the original. Close examination revealed the answer. There it was: the telltale quirk of the flying "i" stood out, a flaw mirrored perfectly on both pieces of paper.

Dan leaned back in the chair, considering the implications of the identical imperfections on the two notes. The one he found last night had been typed on this machine. He couldn't help but wonder if the first note directing him to the maze had also come from the same machine. It seemed likely.

So someone in the household was helping by pointing him in the right direction. Was this person working with the cloaked figure or against it? But who was this individual, and why was he or she doing this?

His eyes flicked to an inbox adorned with a flowery fabric and sitting in the top left corner of the desk. Without hesitation, he rummaged through the papers stacked inside: bills, party invitations, requests for charity donations. Finally, he found what he was looking for.

He picked up the sheet of paper and checked it. It only said "Mother–going to Santa Anita for races. Be back soon. A." There was no date on it. The message had been typed, revealing the familiar "i" of Mrs. Maitland's typewriter, while the "A" was handwritten.

It was odd to Dan the message was typewritten, but perhaps that was how things were done at the Maitlands. After all, his family scribbled notes to each other on whatever was handy. And a single letter — A — is easier to forge than an entire signature. Then there was the lack of a date, but even if there was one, it could have been faked. With care, he returned the note to its original spot in the inbox. So that was inconclusive. The note could have been written by Andrew — or not.

Dan's mind went back to his search of younger Maitland's room last night before and another thought popped into his head. If somebody taking Andrew's clothes didn't bother to remove them from the hangers, perhaps that person didn't bother to take them out of the house, either.

Since Dan had already broken the rule that good house guests don't snoop, he might as well pull out all the stops. Trailed by the Great Danes, he went through the entire house, searching every closet, drawer, and chest he could find. But each unlocked room he scoured yielded nothing.

Then he recalled his conversation with Andrew about the Maitland's famous Halloween gatherings. The costumes; the elaborate disguises. What better place to hide clothes than mixed in with other garments?

Dan made his way to the basement entrance. He reached for the key hanging next to it and unlocked the door, taking a moment to steel himself before turning the knob. He reassured himself that he wouldn't be going into the dungeon. Max and Brutus would remain behind, content to stay on the safety of the first floor. They're the smart ones, Dan thought to himself as he started down.

At the bottom of the steps, the three doors guarding their respective worlds stood before him. Ignoring the door leading to the dungeon, he opened the one directly in front of him. He groped around the edge of the door frame until his fingers found a switch. Naked bulbs on the ceiling burst to life, revealing the furnace and nothing else besides a couple of old chairs. Closing that door, he opened the third and turned on the lights.

He stepped into a long, skinny room, the air tinged with the pungent smell of mothballs. Against one wall ran a tall, metal clothing rack, draped with sheets. As he pulled them off, his eyes widened in surprise at the sight before him — an array of costumes in every shape and size imaginable.

There were jester outfits with colorful bells and floppy hats, vampire capes lined with red velvet, clown suits bursting with vibrant polka dots, beaded 1920s dresses, and even police uniforms, complete with shiny badges. Among them all were things like feathered boas in shades of pink and purple. It was a treasure trove of disguises.

Dan worked his way through the crowded collection, hanger by hanger. He ran his fingers over the sequined edges of costumes, touching tufts of feathered boas and jackets of all kinds. When he made his way to the very back of the small space, he said "bingo".

At the far end of the long rack of outrageous costumes hung Andrew's clothes. Shirts, pants — even the white sweater that Andrew had on when they first met — all still on the same style wooden hangers Dan saw in Andrew's closet.

That settled things in Dan's mind. Despite the note, Andrew did not set off on a last-minute trip to California. Or anywhere else, for that matter, at least under his own steam. Dan needed to deliver this information to Detective Barton.

Dan shut off the light and closed the door. As he climbed upstairs, a rumble of thunder echoed. He wasn't surprised when Max and Brutus were nowhere in sight when he reached the top of the steps. They were finding a place to hide out the storm, no doubt.

The hallway was growing dark as clouds blotted out the sun. Dan grabbed the phone and dialed. He needed to give Paul the information to relay to the detective. The line trilled twice before another click punctuated the silence, signaling an interception. Unseen ears were now privy to the exchange. Again. Dan now had to get Paul out here in person to tell him his findings.

"Case res—" Paul started.

"Paul, buddy, hi!" Dan's voice brimmed with forced cheerfulness.

"Oh, Dan, good, I'm glad you called. I need to tell you—"

Dan cut his brother off again. "Guess what, buddy? Great news! Mrs. Maitland gave the okay for you to come out and stay here."

"She... huh... what?"

"She's in New York and Mrs. Danner is at her sister's, so I have this whole place to myself! Well, except for Romero," Dan enthused. "So she said it was fine for you to come out. And guess what? They have a television set here! Isn't that fantastic?"

"Yeah, but Det—"

"And hey, it'll be pouring all week. That's what the weather forecast says. You can't mow lawns in the rain, now can you, old buddy?" Dan gave a loud, forced laugh.

"Well, no..."

"Tell you what... bring Jake along!" Dan babbled on, the life insurance salesman trying to force the sale to a reluctant prospect. "The more, the merrier, right? That's what Mrs. Maitland said! A direct quote!"

"Danny boy, look, I've been working all day—"

Dan pressed his index finger to the mouthpiece and tapped his nail against it on the next three words. "I need you to see the inside of this place. It's wild, man." He again tapped his nail on the next three words. "I need you to see it to believe it! If you leave now, you should beat the rain here." He held his breath as he waited to see if his brother got the message.

"Okay, you talked me into it," Paul said after a brief pause, a subtle shift in his tone displaying his understanding of Dan. "I'll pick up Jake. We'll be there soon."

"Great, buddy! See you!"

Dan held the phone for a few moments after Paul ended the call. He heard the faint sound of the other extension being placed back on its cradle.

His gaze shifted around the hall, taking in the emptiness. But he knew he was not alone. If Romero and Lang were not present in the house with him, then who was?

Chapter Eleven

The deepening growl of thunder overhead heralded the late afternoon arrival of Paul and Jake, almost drowning out even the jeep's loud engine. Dan stepped out of the front door just as they pulled to a stop under the portico. Wasting no time, Dan ushered them away from the house.

"Let me show you the grounds," he said, guiding them farther from prying walls. "The sun is about to go down."

"Why the grand tour now?" Jake protested, eyeing the black clouds in the sky. "It's about to rain! I don't like walking in the stuff!"

Dan gave a hearty laugh and slapped him on the back. "It's only water, Jake! You won't melt!"

"Something's not right, is it? Were you being listened to on the phone again?" Paul asked once they were beyond earshot of the mansion. Dan nodded. "Anyway, I need to tell you what Steve—"

"Who?" Dan looked puzzled.

"That's what Detective Barton wants us to call him now," Paul answered. He added with meaning, "The same way Mom does."

"Oh." Dan returned an understanding look.

"What I was trying to tell you is that Steve had to close the case," Paul said. "Nothing more can be done without concrete evidence, he says. He said Mrs. Maitland—"

"Told him that Andrew went on a last-minute trip to California and didn't tell her beforehand. He left a note she didn't find for a couple of days," Dan finished.

"Left a note?" Paul replied. "I didn't know that part."

"I read it," Dan said. "That all seemed a little strange to me, but the important thing was Mrs. Maitland accepted the message as legit."

"She showed it to you?" Jake asked.

"Well… no, not exactly. Let's say I, uh, ran across it," Dan hedged.

Paul crossed his arms and arched an eyebrow. "And just how long did it take you to 'run across it', my dear brother?"

"Not long," Dan answered. "Perhaps the reason Mrs. Maitland didn't find the note sooner was because it didn't exist for a couple of days. It only appeared *after* Andrew disappeared. And there's more." Dan told Paul and Jake about the second message leading to his search of Andrew's room, the discovery of the ledger sheet, and its theft.

"Ledger page! Okay, hang on to your hat, Danny boy, because now it's my turn." Paul filled Dan in on the car accident, his finding a ledger sheet and it being stolen along with the notes Dan had given him.

Dan was quiet for a minute while he turned what Paul said to him over in his head. "I wonder if those two pages were duplicates.

The threats about the price attached to them sounded the same. How come two?"

"Oh, and as you ponder that, the number you also, uh, 'ran across' from Lang leads straight to the US Treasury Department," Paul said.

"Why would Lang be calling the Treasury?" Dan asked himself.

"Could be taxes," Jake said.

"Any ideas bubbling in the pot, crime chef?" Paul asked.

"Phone calls listened to, the ledger samples, their theft, notes typed on Mrs. Maitland's own machine, people disappearing..." Dan shook his head and shrugged. "The pot is empty. But I'm getting the feeling I'm an additional ingredient in the recipe." He took a deep breath. "But is this case closed? No, it's not. If Detect... I mean, Steve says he needs solid evidence. Fine. I think I've uncovered some. Come on."

Paul and Jake exchanged glances as Dan strode back to the house. The sky was an ominous canvas of swirling grays and blacks, painting a scene more foreboding than any Frankenstein movie could present. Bristles of electricity charged the air, and the heavens finally split open with a furious roar as the first drops of rain pelted the earth. As the boys reached the cover of the portico, the skies unleashed their full might with a deluge that drummed against the roof with relentless intensity.

"Where are the hounds?" Paul asked as he looked around with caution.

The sound of thunder rattled the house, causing Dan to point toward the sky. "With that noise, they're hiding under a bed somewhere," he said. "Remember Steve said he didn't think Andrew was kidnapped because some of his clothes were missing?"

Paul nodded.

"It's true they were not in his closet, but they are still in the house. Andrew didn't take them with him in a suitcase for a quick jaunt to play the ponies." Opening the front door, Dan led Paul and Jake to the basement room holding the costumes. Flipping on the light to the narrow room, he pointed to the rack of costumes. "They're in here. Down at the other end."

Leaving Jake and Dan at the doorway, Paul squeezed by them and went to the far side of the room. After a few seconds, he held up a pink tutu. "Andrew wore this?"

"No, you dope. Next to it..." Paul's expression stopped him. "Oh, no, don't tell me..."

Paul shrugged. "Okay, I won't."

Dan brushed past his brother. Andrew's clothes were gone. Dan gave a resigned sigh, leaning forward and grabbing the rod with both hands. "The kleptomaniac monk strikes again! The only way not to have something stolen in this house is to nail it down."

A gigantic peel of thunder shook the house to its foundations. The lights flickered.

"Wonderful. The power company may be getting ready to join Max and Brutus under the bed," groused Dan. "I'll show you your rooms, then get my flashlight. It'll probably be needed."

They went up to the hall. Dan closed the basement door and locked it. After a second's consideration, he pocketed the key, then led Paul and Jake to the second floor. He waved a hand toward two rooms across the hall. "Those are yours."

"I'll get the suitcases, Paul," Jake said as he turned to head back downstairs.

"Thanks," Paul replied. He stepped into one of the bedrooms.

Dan went into his bedroom, listening to the thunder rumble outside. Two huge, quivering lumps were under the bedspread. Dan picked up one edge and peeked under the cover, where Max and Brutus had taken refuge from the storm. Dan chuckled at their worried expressions. "Sorry, guys, I can't control the weather," he said as he straightened up and grabbed the flashlight from the dresser.

A blinding bolt of lightning illuminated the room, flooding the room in stark bluish-white. The thunder seemed to waken every echo in the house. The lights flickered and then went out, plunging the room into darkness. A gust of wind blew open the window, the curtains billowing into the air like translucent specters. Dan rushed and closed it, rain drumming against the panes.

"Did you hear that?" Paul stood in the doorway.

"The thunder?" Dan walked to his brother. "Yeah, of course—"

Paul shook his head. "Not that, just before. I thought I heard Jake yell."

"Yell? Yell what?"

"I don't know," Paul said in a worried tone. "Let's find out."

The bright beam of Dan's flashlight cut through the blackness, casting crazy, moving shadows as he and Paul hurried downstairs. After a quick glance around the foyer, they stepped outside, almost tripping over two suitcases dropped on the steps. Dan flashed his light all over the portico while the rain cascaded off the roof in sheets.

The area was empty. The brothers searched around and under the jeep, finding nothing.

"Jake?" Paul called. "Where are you? Jake?"

Another flash of lightning and crash of thunder emphasized the wildness of the night. Dan and Paul looked at each other.

"Where did he go?" Paul asked. "Certainly not out in that storm at night."

"I guess we can add Jake to the list of things that disappear around this place," Dan said.

Chapter Twelve

Dan's brow furrowed as he stood on the front steps, fists planted on his hips. "Jake wouldn't have bolted into this storm," he said, more to himself than to Paul.

"No, I'm sure he wouldn't. At least without a good reason," Paul said, his own voice tinged with frustration. They exchanged a glance that silently acknowledged their shared puzzlement.

"Perhaps he got spooked?" Dan asked.

Paul answered the question with one of his own. "Jake? Spooked?"

"You're right. He wouldn't be. Could he be playing a joke?" Dan asked.

Paul shook his head. "Jake doesn't have much of a sense of humor."

"Then maybe he doubled back in for some reason." Dan jerked his thumb toward the front doors. "But that doesn't explain dumping the suitcases here."

Without another word, they picked up the bags and retraced their steps into the mansion's foyer. Once inside, the only sound was the persistent drumming of rain from outside and the rumble of thunder.

"Before we do anything else, we need more light than this." Dan's voice sounded hollow in the grand space as he held up his flash. "Let's check the living room. There are some candlesticks on the fireplace."

Moving, weird shadows and contours made the familiar unfamiliar in the glare of the flashlight greeted them as they walked into the room. Dan went to an ornate candlestick resting on the mantelpiece. He lifted it and handed it to Paul.

"Here, take this," Dan directed. "Now some matches or ..." He rummaged through an end table drawer until his fingers closed around a lighter. Not an ordinary one, but a novelty one shaped like a gun. The irony of the object wasn't lost on him.

"It's curtains for ya," Dan spoke like a gangster as he aimed the lighter at his brother. With a flick, he ignited the wick of Paul's candle, the flame casting a dancing glow across their faces. He pocketed the lighter and led the way back into the hallway. They hadn't taken more than a few steps into the corridor when a momentary flash of light bouncing from the library doorway stopped them in their tracks. They looked at each other.

Dan put his lips next to Paul's ear. "A flashlight? Who else could be in here?"

"I don't think that it's Jake," Paul whispered back. "We must have company."

Dan nodded in agreement. "But whoever it is may know what happened to him."

The twins tiptoed to the library doors and peered in, pausing as they saw a rogue beam of light reflecting out the connecting door to the morning room. Motioning to his brother, Dan returned to the living room, Paul right behind him.

"It looks like the light is coming from the morning room. There are two ways in," Dan said in hushed tones, "through the library and from the hallway. I'll go through the library, and you come in from the hall. We'll trap whoever it is between us."

Paul gripped a fireplace poker, weighing it in his hand. "Here is a perfect heavy, blunt instrument."

"Well, watch where you swing that thing," Dan said as he pointed at it. "Avoid your dear brother's noggin."

The twins cautiously approached the library door. Dan gave a signal to split up. With a slow exhalation, Paul extinguished his candle, plunging them into darkness once again. He carefully placed the candlestick on the floor and crept towards the hallway door. At the same time, Dan clicked off his flashlight and silently slipped into the room, grateful that the storm outside masked any noise he made as he edged closer to the morning room.

Heart thudding in his chest, Dan pressed himself against the bookcase next to the open door. He took a deep breath and leaned forward just enough to peek around the edge.

There was the unmistakable outline of a man. The silhouette was hunched over Mrs. Maitland's desk, his movements quick and precise as he rifled through the drawers. The flashlight resting on the desktop cast a grotesque shadow of his actions on the wall.

Dan pulled out the lighter, counting on how the dim light could make it confused with a real weapon. He swung into the doorway, aimed his flashlight straight into the figure's face, and switched it on. Romero held up one hand to block the glare.

"Looking for the car keys?" Dan's voice sliced through the silence.

Romero straightened. "What do you want?"

"What I want is to know what you want. Stay where you are and put your hands flat on the desk," Dan commanded. He kept the beam of his light focused directly into Romero's eyes, forcing him to squint against the brightness. After a second, the chauffeur complied. "Thank you. By the way, my brother is behind you. I should mention he's a trained boxer. A good one."

"I appreciate the compliment, my dear brother. Let me add I'm also holding a fat iron fireplace poker in my hand," Paul said. He stood taut with the iron bar raised, ready to strike if necessary. "Perfect for bashing in skulls. You can't jump the two of us at the same time."

"Are you armed?" Romero asked, trying to make out the object in Dan's hand.

"This could be a gun. I've handled them before," Dan answered in a casual tone.

"Three at one time against the Dalton brothers," Paul put in.

"To be accurate, I held a gun in both hands and one was in my belt," Dan said. "But then again, what I'm holding in my hand now may just *look* like a gun. But who knows? You've got a fifty-fifty chance to make a correct guess. Are you feeling lucky?" He paused. "Well, are you?"

A chuckle escaped Romero despite the situation. "Barton warned me about the Case twins."

"Warned you? About us?" Dan's brow furrowed. "What exactly did Detective, uh, Steve say?"

"He told me not to underestimate you two. He was right," Romero answered. "When he came out here to investigate Andrew's missing person report, I informed him of who I was. As a professional courtesy." A ghost of a smile formed on his lips. "He found out Dan was here, so he filled me in on the background about you boys."

Dan let the information sink in, his gaze never wavering from Romero's face, weighing every word for truth. "Professional courtesy? What's that supposed to mean?"

Romero straightened and raised a hand in a placating gesture. "I'm an undercover agent with the United States Treasury Department."

"Treasury, huh?" Paul said, skepticism lacing his tone. "Quick then, what's the number for the office in D.C.?"

"Klamath 5-2000," Romero shot back without missing a beat.

Paul glanced at Dan, nodding. "He's right."

"Any more solid ID than that?" Dan's eyes narrowed.

With deliberate slowness, Romero reached into his hip pocket, easing out his wallet and tossing it onto the polished floorboards before Paul. It landed with a thud. Cautiously, Paul picked up the billfold, thumbing it open to extract an identity card. He held up it to catch the light from Dan's flashlight.

"Yep, he wasn't lying. This guy's a certified G-man," Paul said after a moment of scrutiny. "United States Treasury Department."

"T-man," Dan corrected automatically, his attention fixed on Romero. "T... Treasury."

Dan approached Romero while Paul ran out to the hall and came back with the candle. Dan clicked the lighter and brought the flame to the wick once again.

"Wrong guess," Romero grinned as he watched the flame come to life. He returned his wallet to his pocket and addressed Dan. "I almost told you who I was that night when you found me in the hallway."

"So you were slugged by somebody," Dan said. "The monk?"

Romero shook his head. "I didn't see who it was."

"Okay, now that the formalities are finished," Dan said, "Why are you really here? Why play the role of the family chauffeur?"

"The department received an anonymous tip of more gold not being turned in as required by the Roosevelt executive order. That order is still in force," Romero said, his expression turning serious. "Plus additional information came in later suggesting a disguised Maitland had sneaked back into the country through Canada. His plan was to take the hoard to South America."

"Argentina?" Dan asked.

Romero nodded. He gestured over the desk. "I was checking for any evidence to see if Mrs. Maitland had knowledge of it."

"With a search warrant, I assume," Dan said.

"Of course," Romero replied.

"Do you think these rumors have any connection to Andrew's disappearance?" Dan asked.

Romero shrugged. "I don't know."

"Let's cut the chit-chat," Paul said, his impatience clear. "We have another disappearance to deal with first: Jake."

"Who?" Romero turned to Paul.

"A friend of ours," Paul answered. "He came out here with me, went outside to get our bags, then poof! Gone."

"Paul's right," Dan said. "We know he can't be in the basement because I locked the door when all of us came out. I still have the key."

"That leaves three floors, and three of us. I'll search the third floor. Paul, you take the second and Dan this one," Romero said, taking charge. He checked his watch. "Meet in the foyer in ten minutes."

The group split up, Paul and Romero heading for the staircase while Dan stayed behind to check the French door in the morning room. He jiggled the handle and confirmed that it was still locked tight. Outside, the fierce rain pelted against the windows as Dan made his way through the first floor, checking each room.

The library and dining room were both empty. In the kitchen, pots and pans hung neatly on hooks above a large island, but there was no sign of anyone having been there recently. A glance in the butler's pantry revealed nothing of interest, either. Finally, Dan reached the back door and tried the knob. It was fastened from the inside, just as he had expected.

The servants' quarters came next. Dan discovered nothing of significance in Mrs. Danner's or Romero's rooms. Finally, he moved to the end of the hall and tugged on the last door. With a grumble, he found it was locked. He glanced at his watch. It was time to regroup with the others. With any luck, one of them had uncovered something. He retraced his steps to the foyer.

As he entered the room, Paul came down the stairs, the flickering flame of his lone candle reflecting in his glasses. He shook his head in disappointment, strands of brown hair falling into his eyes as he walked up to his brother.

"Nothing alive up there but Max and Brutus," he said, glancing back towards the steps.

Dan glanced at his watch. "Where's Romero? It shouldn't take this long, even with the attic, to check. The third floor doesn't have many rooms."

They shared a tense silence, letting the time trickle past with only the occasional flash of lightning to disturb it. Finally, with a mutual nod, they both started upstairs.

The gloomy corridor of the top floor stretched before Dan and Paul. Distant thunder punctuated the sound of their cautious footsteps as they opened each door, encountering nothing but shadows and furniture. Room after room offered no clues, no sign of the missing Treasury agent or anything else.

"Here we go again," Paul said at the threshold of the third to last doorway, a note of frustration in his voice.

Dan had tried that door earlier when he was searching for Andrew's clothes, and it was locked. He was about to tell Paul that when his brother swung the door wide and stepped in. Dan followed, muttering to himself "it was locked".

Another bedroom. Dan went to the wardrobe and yanked it open. As if on schedule, a flash of lightning illuminated a skeleton with empty eye sockets, thumbing its nose from inside. Dan let out a startled cry and took a step back.

Paul came next to Dan. "What the —"

"Probably a leftover from one of the Maitland's famous Halloween parties," Dan explained with a wave at the wardrobe's macabre occupant. "Andrew said they decorated the entire house."

"Barrel of laughs, that family is," Paul said under his breath. He stooped to look by the bed. "Wait, I've found something." He straightened up, holding Romero's flashlight.

"Great. Two down, two to go," Dan grimly remarked. He glanced around the room. There were no other doors except the one they came in. He checked the window. "No other way out. The window's locked from the inside and it's a three-story drop. Nowhere to hide other than the wardrobe. And it's taken."

Dan put down the candle and switched on Romero's flash. The pair left the bedroom and tried the last two doors. Neither one budged.

"Did Romero have keys to the place?" Paul asked.

"Sure did. Locked it up tighter than a drum with Mrs. Danner and Mrs. Maitland away," Dan replied.

Paul tilted his head toward a door. "Then did he leave through one of these? Maybe down another staircase? Or lock himself inside until we gave up searching?"

"I've never seen any back stairs." Dan scratched his jaw. "Also, it doesn't add up to him leaving his flashlight behind and locking himself in a room."

"Unless he found what he was looking for," Paul said, a tinge of suspicion coloring his tone. "Gold has a way of changing a man's plans."

Dan grunted a response. He strode toward the stairs with determination. "Okay, let's start over, bottom to top. We must have missed something." He reached the head of the staircase and started down. A loud, long rumble of thunder rattled the house. "Okay, Paul? Paul?"

He stopped and looked over his shoulder. His brother wasn't behind him. He climbed back to the third floor. The corridor was empty. No sign of his twin.

"Paul?" he called. After no answer, he grew irritated. "Look, pal, if this is your idea of a joke, it isn't funny. Knock it off!"

No answer. Only the moaning of the wind and the drumming of the rain reached his ears. Dan shone his light around the hall. The flashlight Paul held rested on the carpet runner. Panic momentarily gripped Dan, realizing he was now alone in the vast, dark house.

No, not alone, he corrected himself. Somebody else was roaming the halls.

Dan swallowed hard. "Three down, one to go. Me." It was time to call the police. The brothers probably should have done that when Jake vanished.

He raced downstairs and headed for the telephone. But when he held the receiver to his ear, he was met with silence. No dial tone, no connection to the outside world. Just the sound of his own breathing echoing in his ear.

In frustration, he slammed down the phone. "Dead. Of course it is." He thought out loud, "The jeep. I'll have to drive to get help."

Jogging down the hall, he stepped through the front door into the stormy night. The vehicle sat under the portico, like a patient horse waiting for its rider. Dan climbed into the driver's seat. He turned the key. The engine cranked, and cranked... and wouldn't start.

"Aw, come on, baby, start, start," Dan urged as he twisted the ignition key again.

The jeep refused to fire. Jumping out, he popped the hood and aimed his flashlight into the engine bay. The beam illuminated the empty space where the distributor cap should have been. It would be impossible to start the jeep without it.

"Someone's playing games!" He slammed down the hood. A moment later, another idea hit. "The Cadillac!"

Dan's feet pounded against the hard floors as he sprinted through the house and into the kitchen. He looked around until he spotted a bright red umbrella hanging from a hook by the back door. He snatched it up and slid open the bolt before reentering the raging storm outside. The wind whipped around him, engaging in a tug-of-war with the edges of the umbrella as he ran towards the carriage house, looming dark and foreboding.

The smell of gasoline and tires permeated the building as Dan entered, shaking off water from his umbrella. He scanned the cluttered space with his flashlight, its beam revealing toolboxes and shelves until it rested on the green Cadillac's trunk.

His heart raced with excitement... but that quickly dissolved when he remembered he didn't have the keys or even knew where they were kept. He wondered if, after reading so many mysteries, he could hotwire the vehicle. But as he approached the limousine, he realized it wouldn't make any difference if he knew where the keys were or not.

The hood was open and a quick glance inside revealed that the distributor cap was also missing. He slammed the hood shut, the sound drowned out by the howling wind outside. It was clear someone didn't want him to leave by car.

"Okay, if I can't drive out of here, I'll walk," Dan said to himself. He'd first check if there were any coats in the foyer's closet before setting out.

The downpour drummed against his umbrella as he sprinted back to the mansion. His feet splashed through deepening puddles, the rain soaking the bottom of his pants. Finally reaching the kitchen, he shut the door and locked it behind him. Tossing aside the soggy umbrella, he rushed towards the entry with water squelching in his sneakers. Every step felt like he was a wildebeest, fleeing from unseen predators cloaked in the darkness.

A burst of frigid air smacked into him as he hurried past the living room. He paused and peered in, momentarily blinded by a jagged bolt of lightning that illuminated the room. The French doors were open, but he distinctly remembered they were latched when he checked earlier.

He dashed to close and lock them again. But those windows being open and no wet footprints on the floor could only mean one thing: somebody inside the house must have gone outside.

And could be waiting for him in the night.

Dan hesitated to try to think of another option. No, his only choice was to brave the storm and get to a neighboring house. Hopefully, he could elude anybody outside.

Rushing into the foyer, he quickly passed by the suit of armor. Its joints let out a metallic groan that pierced through the sound of rain and wind. Its raised battleaxe slipped from its gauntlet and fell to the ground with a loud thud. Dan jumped away, feeling the swoosh of air as the weapon landed right where he had been standing moments ago.

"Great," he said, eyeing the armor with suspicion. "Now even the house is trying to kill me."

Shaken, Dan turned to the closet nearby and opened it. His hands fumbled over the coats and jackets until they found what he hoped was stored inside. Relief washed over him as he pulled out a heavy raincoat. It would shield him from the storm's wrath outside, so at least the elements would not claim him this night. He started to slip on the coat, then stopped.

A scream sliced through the darkness.

Chapter Thirteen

Consciousness seeped back into Paul's mind, a thick fog evaporating from his brain and his head pounding. His eyelids felt heavy as they fluttered open, his vision met with complete darkness. It was as if a blindfold had been placed over his eyes.

Paul tried to take a deep breath to clear his head, but couldn't. Layers of duct tape sealed his mouth, making it impossible for him to call for help or even scream. The sticky material also bound his wrists and ankles, cutting off circulation and causing numbness to spread through his limbs.

Unable to move, he sat on a wooden floor with the rough surface of a post rubbing into his back, his hands secured behind it. He fought with the unyielding grip of the duct tape, but it refused to yield.

He calmed his body, allowing his muscles to relax as he tried to understand the situation. Leaning his head against the post, his brain churned to make sense of everything. What happened to him, and where was he? The last he remembered was standing in the hallway.

His brother was walking toward the stairs, spouting off something about searching the house again. Paul recalled thinking it was a stupid plan because they probably had overlooked nothing the first time. Before he could say that, somebody reached from behind him and pressed a cloth over his face, drenched in a liquid with a sweet aroma. An arm locked around his throat, choking him. He had no clear idea of what was happening as somebody dragged him backward through a doorway... then lights out.

Okay, he got jumped. Now where was he?

The rain drummed just above his head, a sign that he was likely close to the roof. Utter darkness surrounded him, trapping him inside a thick, suffocating blanket. Straining his eyes, he searched for any glimmer of light or shape that might reveal his location. In the distance, a lighter shade of dark formed a rectangular outline — almost like a lighthouse in the sea of blackness. It could be a window, he thought. It was the only visible object in the vast emptiness — his sole point of reference.

Paul jumped at a loud thunderclap and a brilliant flash of lightning illuminating the room, allowing him to catch a brief glimpse of his surroundings. There were old wooden beams, a slanted ceiling, and the post to which he was tied. Various objects cluttered the surrounding floor, including trunks, chairs, boxes, and picture frames. His location was now confirmed — he was in the attic of the mansion.

In the midst of the pounding rain, another sound caught his attention: a faint rustling and shuffling emerging from the shadows.

Was he not alone in this trapped space? He hoped it wasn't a rat. Those creatures gave him the creeps.

Paul attempted to shout through the tape, gagging him, but his words came out muffled and unintelligible. A response came almost immediately, a mumble bouncing off the walls, not understandable, but it was human. Somebody else shared the attic with him.

"Jake?" he tried again, the name coming out with a stifled grunt.

Three distinct syllables echoed back, distorted and unclear.

Frustration mounted in Paul. He needed to know who the other person was up here with him. "Who?"

The trio of sounds repeated in the same way. Then Paul got it — Ro-me-ro.

"Ro-me-ro?" Paul called out, pronouncing each part of the name with as much clarity as he could muster through the gag.

"Uh-huh," came the voice again.

Another brilliant flare of lightning lit up the attic, and for an instant, Paul could see his fellow captive. Romero, a mirror of Paul's own situation, bound to a neighboring structural post.

Paul thrashed against the unforgiving grip of the duct tape once more. His muscles strained and burned in his attempt to break free. The sticky adhesive clung to his skin like a second layer. He gritted his teeth and pulled with all his might. The tape seemed to stretch, only a bit. But it wasn't enough.

He groaned, dropping his head on his chest.

Shifting, he tried to find a more bearable position. Instead, his forearm grazed along something sharp. He winced, then he realized it was a nail sticking out from the post he was tied to. It would be his luck that it was likely rusty, and he'd end up with tetanus. But another thought came into his mind. The nail may prove useful to him.

Grimacing with determination, Paul twisted his arms at an uncomfortable angle to place the tape against the pointed tip of the nail. He started to saw back and forth, feeling the rough metal grind against the tape and, he hoped, wear down its layers.

The sound of scrapping fabric mixed with the rain and thunder as he worked to weaken the bindings on his wrists.

***

Dan tried to convince his brain the scream was not real. After experiencing weird things in this house, from people vanishing to discovering hidden identities to a battleaxe trying to cleave him in two, so it makes sense his nerves were on edge. It was reasonable for him to question what he heard. He nodded. Yes, it must have been his imagination. Maybe it was only the wind, he thought. Causing something metal to squeak back and forth.

"Well, it should get oiled," Dan said to himself with grim humor.

Yeah, it was only the wind. Howling down the chimney. That was the usual explanation given in the movies — just before something horrible happened. He kicked that thought out of his head.

The scream was nothing more than a product of his mind. Or at least, that's what the truth must be. He started tugging on the raincoat again, determined to bring help.

Through the sound of the pouring rain and rumbling thunder came a sharp snap and another muffled cry. It was one of pain, but the person was trying their best to choke it down. Dan froze with the coat halfway on. He shook his head. No, that couldn't have —

The sounds repeated.

Okay, those were definitely real, Dan decided with resignation. He shrugged off the raincoat and stood silently, straining to hear if there were any more noises. There wasn't an encore performance.

He would have to track down the source. Grabbing his flashlight, he made his way toward the hallway. As he passed by the suit of armor, he picked up the fallen battleaxe. "I'll give this back when I'm finished with it," he assured the knight.

Step by step, he crept through the darkened house, brandishing the battleaxe in one hand, the flashlight in the other. His breath caught with each creak of the floorboards. He checked every room on the ground level — living room, dining room, morning room, library, and kitchen. No signs of anyone or anything that could have caused the alarming noises. Back in the hallway, he thought about what he heard. They didn't seem to come from upstairs, but they had a muffled quality, as though they came from...

He looked down at the floor. One place left to search the dungeon. Going to the basement door, he pressed his ear against the cold wood. Faint sounds emerged from the depths of the house. He strained to make sense of them, but they were indecipherable. Were people talking, perhaps?

He leaned the battleaxe against the wall and his hand closed around the doorknob. It refused to turn. Then a frustrated sigh escaped his lips. He locked it earlier. He had forgotten in the excitement. With a groan at his stupidity, he pulled the key from his pocket and inserted it into the lock.

Then he thought about something. How did someone manage to go down there when the door was locked and he held the key? It didn't take him long to answer that one. A duplicate must be floating around somewhere.

The lock snapped, and the door creaked open. Dan paused at the top of the stairs, peering into the abyss below. His flashlight beam was a small circle of white, punching a feeble hole into the blackness. But another light seeped out from under the dungeon door at the bottom of the steps. It flickered, orange and yellow and red... like fire. Just what he needed: the place was burning on top of everything else going on.

Picking up the battleaxe, Dan hurried down the stairs. He pushed open the heavy door with his shoulder and stepped into the dungeon. He stopped dead, taking in a bizarre scene before him. It was unlike anything he had ever seen before.

Chapter Fourteen

Paul's shoulders ached with strain and fatigue as he sawed the duct tape over the nail. Up and down. Up and down. His breath came in quick breaths of the thick air, dusty with the scent of disuse that permeated the attic. A bead of sweat trickled down his temple. He paused a second to rest, then fought with the bonds again.

Nothing. There seemed to be no change in the duct tape's grip.

But he had to keep going, even though he didn't want to. It was like sometimes when he was in the ring. He needed to stay with it, keep punching, and not give up. His job started again. The rasping sound of duct tape against the nail grated on his nerves.

Without warning, the tension gave way. Paul twisted his wrists, and the tape ripped apart. He laughed — or tried to through the gag — in triumph. The drumming of the rain on the roof sounded like applause. His arms were free.

He tore the tape from his mouth, leaving a tingling sensation around his lips. His voice was hoarse as he whispered into the darkness, "Romero, my hands are free."

But now came a new challenge: the tape binding his ankles. The black void surrounding him was impenetrable, and he couldn't see the tape at all. He got hold of it, but it refused to yield to his fumbling fingers.

A flash of lightning tore through the gloom, illuminating the attic for a brief, blazing moment. Paul's eyes locked onto the face of a stern man staring back at him. The old photograph was in a frame hanging from the post opposite him. Its glass covering beckoned as a potential tool in his bid for freedom.

Darkness reclaimed the space once more. Paul rolled to his side and kept rolling until he reached the post he had been aiming for. Struggling to get up, he climbed to his knees and stretched up for the photo. His fingers only brushed the bottom.

He hugged the post and pulled himself up, hitting his forehead on the frame. Using his head, he jerked the photograph up. It fell off its nail and shattered on the ground with a satisfying crash.

Paul let himself down and felt for the frame, carefully picking up a shard of glass, its sharp and icy surface against his skin. He used it as a makeshift knife to cut through the tape that bound his ankles together, at last releasing his feet.

"I'm loose. Romero, make noise so I can find you. I can't see a thing," Paul said. A shuffling answered him, followed by a soft thumping. "Got it. Okay, here I come."

Paul didn't want to chance falling over any of the attic clutter, so he army-crawled across the dusty floor. He smacked his head into a large trunk. Grunting, he pushed it aside and continued his slow progress towards Romero's pounding. He was wondering if somehow headed in the wrong direction when his hand fell on the treasury agent's foot.

Patting his hand, Paul worked his way up Romero's leg and torso, reaching his shoulder. He then moved down his arm and found his wrists.

"I'll try not to cut you with the glass, but..." Paul said. Romero gave a muffled "okay."

Using a shard, Paul began cutting through the layers of duct tape that bound Romero's hands.

***

The flames from the brazier flickered in the dungeon's corner, casting dancing shadows on the cold stone walls. Andrew stood, chained to a set of manacles, facing one wall, three angry welts across his bare back. Despite his situation, he still wore his usual bored expression as he gazed at Dan.

A stocky man, wearing khaki work clothes and a cap pulled tight over his crew cut, was at the rear of Andrew, whip in hand. From next to the rack, the mysterious monk watched with arms crossed as the scene unfolded in front of him.

For a second, Dan was so shocked he couldn't find his voice. When he did, he sounded like his mother when she discovered the brothers roughhousing. His words echoed through the stone chamber, bouncing off the walls. "What on earth is going on here?"

Before he could say anything else, rough hands seized him from behind. They pinned his arms in back of him with an iron grip, halting any attempt at resistance. Dan struggled against his unknown captor, but it was like fighting the roots of an ancient tree. The battleaxe and flashlight clanged and clattered to the floor.

Andrew spoke to Dan, sounding as if making introductions at a dinner party. "I'm afraid I'm not acquainted with the other two gentlemen, the one with the whip and the one who has hold of you. But allow me to introduce our hooded friend here. That would be Tony Dietz. He was once my father's partner, and now is the esteemed sole owner of the Beaumont Foundry." He nodded to the two other men. "Those two are the only ones I've seen or talked to. But Dietz here, dressed like some two-bit comic book villain, was always lurking around, passing notes to his two goons on what to say. He assumed that wouldn't permit me to recognize his voice or him. He was wrong."

The cowled figure didn't move or make a sound.

"Oh, come on, Dietz, give it up," Andrew said in exasperation. "I know it's you under there. You wore that costume every year without fail for the Halloween party. Skulked through the house, calling yourself 'The Phantom Monk' or some such drivel. Very original. As for these others, I'd wager they're just some of the foundry's finest. Aren't you lads?" He cast a sardonic glance toward the other men. "I hope at least Dietz is paying you well."

After a moment, the monk reached up and pulled away the cowl of the monk's robe, then removed the mask. As the outfit fell away like a shed skin, it revealed Tony Dietz. He was short, but his pudgy frame seemed to bristle with anger. A fringe of black hair circled the gleaming dome of his bald head. His face was pasty white, emphasizing a pair of eyes that burned with fury. He faced Dan.

"Who are you?" The question came sharp, commanding, and threatening, despite Dietz' high-pitched voice.

"I'm a friend of Andrew's." Dan met Dietz's eyes with a defiant stare.

"Andrew has no friends," Dietz sneered.

"He does now," Dan shot back, his tone edged with steel.

Dietz snapped off a disbelieving laugh. "Do you want me to tell you who you are?"

Dan fired back. "That might be nice since it seems I don't have any idea."

"Fine, I'll tell you who you are! You're Andrew's accomplice!" Dietz jabbed a stubby finger toward Dan.

The implicit accusation behind the gesture was clear. Somehow, Dan had become ensnared in this twisted mess.

"Me? An accomplice!" Dan couldn't believe what he was hearing.

Andrew's voice remained composed as he addressed Dan. "Dietz has gotten it into his thick skull that I'm blackmailing him."

"You are a blackmailer!" Dietz spat the words like venom, stepping closer to where Andrew was restrained. "How long do you think you can play dumb, Andrew? You're the only one who could have stolen those documents!" He jerked his head toward Dan. "With his help."

"Dietz," Andrew said with a weary indifference, "I have told you and your goons repeatedly that I have no idea what you are talking about. I don't know a thing about your imaginary papers."

"You think you are quite clever, don't you?" Dietz's voice brimmed with disgust. "You wrote the letters... those demands of payment for not providing certain information to the police. However, you slipped up a few times. You left subtle hints in them, revealing your true identity." He tapped his temple with one finger. "You see, I'm smarter than you. I put together those clues and they all pointed to the same conclusion. You! You have those documents, and they are hidden somewhere in this house!"

"How many times do I have to tell you, I don't—" Andrew started to say.

"Shut up!" Dietz yelled. "I'm not losing everything I've worked for so long and so hard to some lazy, worthless bum."

"You worked for," Andrew scorned.

"Yes, I worked for!" Dietz fired back. His voice dripped with contempt. "Which is more than I can say for you! You only came to the foundry when you needed money from your father."

Andrew remained silent, but even in the flickering gloom, Dan picked up regret passing over the younger Maitland's face.

"You never cared about him or the foundry... you were only interested in your pleasure. The parties, the horse racing. You never helped him. Never even offered to." Dietz all but thumped his hand against his chest. "I did it all. I made that business into what it is today. Me. Your father would have closed down a thousand times over if I hadn't been there! I figured out that since I was running the business, it was already my own. So I made it mine… all mine."

"Not by legal means," Andrew added.

"Ha! There! Another mistake!" Dietz said with relish. "There is only one way you could make that statement. With knowledge uncovered in those documents."

"Here we go again," Andrew said. "I know nothing about any papers."

"No? What about the ledger?" Dietz smiled, the hunter laying a trap.

"Ledger? What ledger? You're speaking in riddles," Andrew dismissed.

Dietz waved at the man holding the whip. "Gus was on his way here with the last blackmail letter, which contained a ledger page… 'As a sample,' the note said. In his excitement, he was speeding and drove off the road. Gus lost track of the paper during the accident, but fortunately retrieved it." He pointed at Dan. "This is where your accomplice comes in."

"I do?" Dan asked, puzzled. "I'm with Andrew. I do not know what you're talking about."

"You rescued Gus from the car," Dietz said

"Me?" Dan was incredulous.

"Lying won't help." He turned to Gus. "Is this the kid who pulled you out of the wreck?"

Gus nodded.

Dan opened his mouth to say that it was his brother, but thought better of it.

Dietz spoke to Dan as if he were summing up a case as a district attorney. "The letter and ledger page were found at your home. Your address was written on the calendar in the kitchen, with instructions to Romero about picking you up. Gus went to your house and stole the papers back.

Later, it appears you removed copies of those same items from Andrew's room. I took those from you. Remember our encounter outside in the hall? Perhaps you were unaware that Gus had already retrieved the originals, or you were afraid the water ruined them. So you were preparing to send me another set. It also seems logical that you mailed the initial ones, considering Andrew was... under our care at the time."

"I was told to search Andrew's room, by an anonymous note!" Dan blurted out.

"An anonymous note?" Dietz snorted in disbelief. "And you blindly followed the directions written in an unsigned missive? And I am supposed to buy that?"

"Well... yeah. It's true," Dan said, realizing how stupid it sounded, "but I didn't know what I was going to find."

"That answer is almost as bad as saying you don't know what I'm talking about." Dietz faced Andrew. "Your turn. Would you care to explain why an identical copy of the ledger page and letter was found in your room? Can you solve that little riddle for me?"

Andrew's carefully crafted facade crumbled. All of his denials about his knowledge of the letters disappeared in a puff of smoke, leaving behind an expression of defeat etched onto his face. "I don't know," he said in a quiet voice.

Dan flinched as the whip lashed across Andrew's back. The young Maitland cried out in pain.

"Let me give 'em a couple of dozen more," Gus growled. "He'll talk."

Dietz released an annoyed sigh and raised a restraining hand to Gus. He spoke to Andrew. "You refused to negotiate. Starvation didn't break you. So now it is time to move on to other measures." Dietz waved a hand around the dungeon. "You often told me how this is your favorite room in the house. It is time to put it to its original purpose. Although I would enjoy allowing Gus here to give you the full treatment, I think we won't use the toys here on you... yet."

He took a couple of steps toward the young man. "I must grudgingly admit that you have stood up to more than I expected. But how much do you think your accomplice here can endure? How long can you watch? How about it, Andrew?" He flashed a wintry smile to Dan. "I should warn you, though. Based on how selfish Andrew is, it may be quite a while before he changes his mind."

Without waiting for an answer, Dietz gestured to the foundry workers, pointed at Dan, and then gave the command. "Tie him on the rack."

Chapter Fifteen

Paul continued his work, slicing through the tape bindings around Romero's wrists. He cut through each strip until the last one finally gave way under the sharp edge of the glass. With a swift motion, he pulled the bindings from Romero's wrists. The treasury agent wasted no time in ripping off the gag that had silenced him.

"Here, be careful. It's sharp." Grabbing Romero's hand, Paul placed the jagged shard in his palm. Romero took the makeshift blade and started sawing through the restraints around his ankles.

"Thanks," Romero said.

Paul flashed a grin. "Anytime. That's what friends are for." Romero let out a laugh as he worked to free his feet. "How did we get stuck up here? What happened?"

"Chloroform," Romero said between the sound of rasping as the slivered piece of glass sliced through the tape. "Someone got the jump on each of us with chloroform-soaked rags. Knocked us clean out."

"The last thing I remembered was that I was on the third floor..." Paul started.

"Which is why it was easy for whoever it was to drag our unconscious bodies up here," Romero said as his binds fell away. "Even if we weren't completely out yet, the chloroform made us less of a problem until they got us out of the way."

"How long were we out?" Paul stood and helped Romero to his feet.

"We can't be sure. Chloroform's effects are wildly variable outside a controlled environment, like in a medical office." Romero tossed the glass aside. It tinkled as it broke on the floor. "But given the lingering grogginess? I'd say no more than thirty minutes. No more."

"Okay. Half an hour down the drain. We need to find Jake and Dan — now," Paul looked around. "Where are the stairs? It's so dark up here. I can't see anything."

"Over this way, I think. To our right," Romero said. "Follow the posts. Go from one to the other. Grab my shoulders and stay in the back of me."

Paul did so. Without another word, the two headed toward where they hoped the staircase was, Romero's hands outstretched as they groped through the pitch black in a bizarre conga line.

"Here's one," Romero said. "On we go." They moved on to the next one, then the next one, guiding them through the darkness of the attic. The rain had finally stopped, the only sounds were dripping of water running off the room and their footsteps echoing in the stale air.

"Wait, I got it... the railing," Romero said.

They felt their way downstairs until they reached the door. It didn't budge.

Romero rattled the doorknob. "Locked."

"Dan told me you had the keys," Paul said.

Paul heard Romero pat his pants pockets. "They took them." He was quiet for a moment. "I guess we have to do this the old-fashioned way... break through. The door frame — the area around the handle or lock — it's usually the weakest part. See if you can get an idea of where the lock is."

Reaching down, Paul touched the knob. "Found it."

"Alright, we'll alternate kicks. Aim for the handle and start kicking. I'll go first," Romero said.

Side by side, the two lashed out with well-aimed kicks, the dull thuds of their shoes against wood marking time. Once, twice, a dozen times, until at last, the lock yielded with a splintering crack. Pulling the door open, they stepped into the corridor from the confines of the attic, catching their breath.

"Mrs. Maitland probably won't like us damaging her door," Paul said.

"She can take it out of my pay," Romero replied.

Paul laughed, then spotted the flashlight on the floorboards where he dropped it. He picked it up and flicked it on. "Dan said he was going to start searching the house again from the first floor."

"We'll do the same thing," Romero nodded.

"Might as well. Hopefully, Dan hasn't been snatched, too," Paul said.

The two started down the hallway at a jog.

***

The dank air of the dungeon pressed down on Dan like a slab of concrete. He lay tied, stretched upon the rack, each muscle taut with apprehension, a ragged gag stuffed in his mouth. His eyes darted among the others in the room. Released from the manacles, Andrew stood next to the device, his hands bound behind him.

"Where did you hide those documents, Andrew?" Dietz's voice was as cold and unforgiving. He rested his hand on the torture device, a silent threat that needed no words.

"Dietz, how many times do I need to tell you? How stupid can you be?" Andrew answered. "I didn't steal those papers, and they are not hidden in this house."

"Shall I proceed?" Dietz waved a hand over Dan. "It's up to you."

Although Andrew's face remained as expressionless as always, but his eyes blazed with defiance. "You wouldn't dare."

"I wouldn't?" Dietz smirked. He nodded to the hulking forms of Gus and Mac, the other man. They took their positions at the wheels at the end of the rack, their hands grasping the ancient wooden spokes. They waited for the order.

"If you hurt my new friend, Dan, I swear I'll haunt you for the rest of your days. I will get my revenge." Andrew's voice was as flat and unemotional as if ordering from a restaurant menu. That lack of emotion, the almost matter-of-fact tone, only added to the ominous quality of his threat.

For a moment, an unmistakable shadow of fear crossed Dietz's features, but it vanished quickly. He regained his composure and offered an indulgent smile, the parent humoring a foolish remark from a child. He faced Gus and Mac. "Turn it."

The wheels creaked, and the ratchets clacked as they snapped into place. The ropes became taut, pulling up on Dan's wrists. The strain on his joints mounted and pain shot through his limbs. He grimaced, his body contorting in silent protest.

"Stop! Stop it! Alright... I'll talk! I'll tell you!" Andrew's voice cracked like a whip across the dungeon.

Dietz signaled, and the men released the pressure. Dan exhaled as he reassembled into one piece. But the threat still hung in the air as Dietz faced Andrew. "There. I knew you would respond to reason. Well?"

"The letters..." Andrew began. Before he could continue, distant voices came from upstairs.

"Dan! Jake!"

"Down here! We're down here!" Andrew's shout tore from his throat, desperate and loud.

***

Paul grabbed Romero's arm as they halted abruptly at the top of the stairs. The sound of a distant voice hovered like a ghost. "Did you hear that?"

Romero gave a quick nod and the two of them rushed downstairs to the foyer. The agent tapped Paul on the shoulder and gestured towards the living room doors. They entered but discovered nothing out of the ordinary. The same was true for the library; there was nothing to be found. As they re-entered the hallway, Paul suddenly stopped and directed Romero's attention to the basement door. It was ajar.

"Dan locked that tight earlier," Paul said. "He must have gone down there for some reason. Maybe to start his search there."

Romero placed a palm on the door and pushed it open. He pointed to the flickering light coming from under another door at the base of the stairs.

"Careful," he cautioned, his hand raised in a silent command. "We don't know what's going on down there. It could be nothing, or…"

Paul gave a small nod of acknowledgment, then turned off his flashlight. The two made their way downstairs with caution, testing each step before putting their full weight on it. When they reached the bottom, they stopped and strained to listen for any sound of movement from the far side of the door. Romero placed his hand on the doorknob, then leaned in, placing his lips next to Paul's ear.

"We go in on three," he whispered. "One… two… three!"

The two burst into the room. The dungeon greeted them with emptiness and shadows, except for a solitary figure stretched on the rack, a monk's habit thrown over him like a shroud.

"Dan?" Paul's voice was both a question and a plea. A muffled response came from under the cloth.

Paul raced to the rack and tugged the robe away, uncovering his brother. Paul pulled out the gag. He untied Dan's hands while Romero worked on his feet. "Are you alright, buddy?"

Dan swallowed. "Yeah. You got here just in time. If you were any later, I would have been the taller twin. That would have made me the upper Case."

Romero stopped for a second and spoke to Paul. "What did he just say?"

"Sometimes strange things come out of my brother's mouth." Paul finished undoing the ropes. "You get used to it after a while."

"Sorry... nerves," Dan said

Paul helped Dan sit up, his legs dangling over the edge of the rack. "Thanks." He took a deep breath and let it out before going on. "The mastermind behind all of this is Tony Dietz. He took control of the Beaumont Foundry from Maitland by less than legal means, it sounds like. He has a couple of henchmen working for him, probably from the foundry Gus and Mac. I didn't get their last names." He faced Paul. "Gus was the one you pulled from the wreck, and he then found out our address. He stole the papers from your room. I suppose he didn't know we were a matched set."

He turned back to Romero. "Dietz believes Andrew got his hands on incriminating documents concerning how Dietz took over the business. He thinks Andrew hid them in this house and is blackmailing him. He also suspects me to be Andrew's accomplice. I guess I was in the wrong place at the wrong time. Anyway, Dietz kidnapped Andrew and was trying to force him to tell him the location of the missing papers. That's why Dietz brought Andrew here. He planned to use the dungeon for its original purpose." Dan rolled his shoulders. "Which he started practicing on me. Dietz wore this," he held up the robe before tossing it to the floor, "as a disguise when he searched the house for the documents. That's all I've got for you."

"That's plenty," Romero said in admiration.

"Andrew a blackmailer? Do you believe it?" Paul asked.

Dan shrugged. "I'm not sure. Andrew was about to spill everything to Dietz when your shouts reached us. That was Andrew who yelled back."

Romero's gaze darted around the dank room. "Where did Dietz take Andrew? Which way did they go?"

"I don't know." Dan shook his head. "When Andrew heard you guys and called out, Dietz... he just threw that stupid robe over me." He pointed to the discarded monk's habit crumpled on the stone floor. "All I heard after that was the sound of movement and scuffling."

"I need to get an APB out on Dietz and his goons." Romero started to leave.

Dan massaged his wrists where the ropes had bitten into the skin. "The phone's dead. Oh, plus both the jeep and the Cadillac are disabled."

"Perfect," Romero said under his breath. "I'll head over to the next estate. Their phone has to be working." He raced toward the door.

"Be careful," Paul called after him, but Romero was already gone, his footsteps echoing as they climbed the staircase.

"Where were you two?" Dan asked.

"One or two of the Dietz' goons used chloroform on us," Paul said.

"Gus or Mac," Dan put in.

"Alright, let's use proper names. Mac and/or Gus used chloroform on us and carted us to the attic. Tied us up," Paul said. "Dan, we have to find Jake."

"He's probably trussed up somewhere like you and Romero were." Dan checked over his shoulder as if expecting shadows to move. "I'm sure he's pretty uncomfortable but safe for now. We need to get after Dietz first. If we lose his trail, we'll lose Andrew, too. And Dietz knows we're on to him now. Look, Jake is strong and can take care of himself. We can't afford a wild goose chase after him when all the bad guys could be slipping away."

"I don't like it, but I guess you're right." Paul scanned the creepy room. "I don't get it. How did all those people get out of here? What, four of them? Nobody passed us on the stairs."

"There must be another way out," Dan said.

Paul crossed his arms and gave a snort. "No kidding, Sherlock."

Dan hopped off the rack and started walking around the room. He faced Paul and snapped his fingers. "This estate was built to resemble a castle. The architecture, the hedge maze, this dungeon..." He gestured at the walls. "And what self-respecting dungeon doesn't have a secret passage?"

Paul cast his eyes over every crevice and corner. He threw up his hands. "Well, where is it?"

Dan leaned toward his sibling and gave a sickening, sweet smile. "That's why it's called 'secret', Einstein."

"Hardy-har-har," Paul said. He sighed. "Well, where do we start? Just pick a wall, any wall?"

Dan fixed his gaze on the floor. A glimmer of light reflected off a layer of mud and water.

"Look." He pointed to the flagstones. "It looks like someone came in from the storm outside. You know how Mom yells at us for tracking muddy footprints all over the house. Let's look for areas that are the wettest, or any unusual spots that have water. Even if dried up, there still would be mud. Anything like that."

Dan picked up his dropped flashlight. Using the two, the brothers traced the wet trail on the floor. It became less pronounced near the dungeon door. "They didn't go this way," Paul said, more to himself than to Dan.

Their search continued, at last bringing them to the iron maiden. Its grotesque form loomed like a silent sentinel in the twisting shadows of the flames in the brassier. Puddles of mud and water pooled around the base.

"Here," Dan said, grabbing onto the iron maiden, "this has to be it. This thing must open or slide or something."

Paul's hands clenched the icy metal as he joined Dan in the struggle. They strained their muscles, pushing, pulling, and tugging. Finally, the iron maiden yielded to their efforts.

"Got it!" Paul said. "Hinges are on this side."

They wedged their fingers between the wall and one edge of the iron maiden, then yanked. It swung open like a door to reveal a dark corridor stretching beyond their sight. The muddy trail continued into the dark.

"One secret passage." Dan swept out one arm and bowed. "After you, sir."

"Why, thank you very much. So very kind." Paul nodded his head.

The brothers stepped into the hidden passageway, their footsteps reverberating off the stone floors. The walls closed in around them. They came upon an archway on their left and stopped, flashing their lights into its darkness. Just on the other side stood a narrow staircase, its steps angling upwards. The twins looked at each other.

"Looks like those go to the other floors," Dan said as they played their flashlights on the treads, "probably meant for servants when this house was built. I wouldn't be surprised if Dietz somehow got a hold of the keys for the doors for every floor. Then he used the stairs to sneak around in his monk getup, searching for those documents. That's how he disappeared the times I saw him. Slipped through the stairway door and locked it behind him. The two goons must have done the same."

"Could he have escaped on them now?" Paul asked. "Used them for his getaway?"

Dan shook his head. "I don't think so. Check out the steps. There's a little water on them, but they're mostly dry. It looks like just one set of muddy shoe prints."

"Probably one of the goons after taking care of Romero and me," Paul said. "It doesn't look like the entire crowd used them."

They pressed on, the passage growing tighter and more claustrophobic, like the belly of a slumbering snake. Paul gasped.

"What?" Dan asked.

Paul waved his hand. "Cobwebs. I hate walking into those things."

The trail of mud and puddles grew thicker. The air became heavy and damp, with an earthly smell.

"It's like being buried alive down here," Dan said.

"That's what I like about you," Paul remarked. "You always look on the bright side."

"That's me," Dan said in a lilting voice. "A fluttering bluebird of happiness, spreading joy and cheer wherever I fly."

"I'm going to barf," Paul groaned.

The narrow passage took a sudden left turn and led to a flight of stone stairs. The steps glistened with a layer of mud and water.

"This is it," Paul said, his voice low. "The exit."

The twins ascended the moss-covered stairs. They abruptly ended at a solid wall, blocking the way forward. A chilly breeze whispered through the cracks, carrying with it the clean scent of rain.

"Feel that?" Paul asked, pressing his palm along the surface, feeling the faint movement of air. "There's the outside on the other side of this." He flashed the light around the stone barrier. "I can't see a catch."

"Push!" Dan set his shoulder to the chilly stone, joined by Paul.

With a strong effort, they heaved against the barrier. It gave way with unexpected ease, dumping the brothers onto another hard floor.

"Must be counterweighted," Dan said as he sat up, brushing off his hands.

"Where are we?" Paul asked.

Dan stood, picked up his flashlight, and looked around. "In the crypt."

Paul also got up. "Crypt! This joint is so—" A muffled voice and scrapping came from behind them. "Sounds like we disturbed somebody's eternal rest."

The two spun around. The light beams landed on a coffin niche where Jake lay bound and gagged. Dan rushed over.

"Jake!" Paul pulled out the gag. "Are you alright?"

"Yeah," Jake twisted, so his tied hands could be reached.

"What happened?" Paul untied Jake's wrists while Dan took his feet.

"I was getting the suitcases out of the jeep when I saw two guys," Jake rasped out once free, rubbing the area where the ropes had bitten into his skin. "They were forcing someone else into this place. I shouted to you both, then ran over to stop them." He hopped off the shelf. "But there was another person I didn't see. Somebody came up behind me and jammed a cloth over my face." He threw a punch in the air. "Bam! I was down for the count."

"Did anybody else come out through here?" Dan pointed to the secret door.

Jake nodded. "You bet. It was a regular parade. Same guys I saw earlier, I think, but they were carrying the third one between them. Must have knocked him cold. And one other guy. Bald."

"The cargo would be Andrew. They probably gave him the chloroform treatment Jake, Romero, and I got," Paul said to Dan.

"When did you see them?" Dan's question sliced through the chill air of the crypt.

"Not long before you two tumbled in. Ten minutes tops, maybe," Jake said.

"Did you see which way they went?" Dan walked to the wrought-iron gate and looked out.

"To the right," Jake jerked his head in the direction.

Dan unlatched the gate and opened it. Paul joined him, shining his flashlight on the ground. It lit up messy, trampled mud at the bottom of the tomb steps.

"Is there a road that way?" Paul's light traced the footprints leading off into the night.

"No roads. They're headed for the canal instead," Dan said.

"Canal?" Paul peered into the darkness.

"It's an old industrial one that runs between the river and a lake. It's down the hill past the tennis court." Dan pointed. "Dietz must be using a boat."

"A boat!" echoed Paul.

"Dietz may be as smart as he thinks he is," Dan said. "He didn't want to park a car on the road or use the driveway. Too much chance of being spotted, particularly if he was trundling Andrew around with him. So he used a boat to bring Andrew here, and now he's trying to slip away the same way."

"In this weather?" asked Jake in disbelief.

"Why not? A boat in a storm? Few people would even think about that... so that's why Dietz is doing it. He could moor anywhere along the river and then transfer to a car. It could be a clean getaway." Dan thought for a moment. "They must be slowed down by carting around Andrew's dead weight. We may still catch them! Come on!"

Chapter Sixteen

T he boys' sneakers splashed as they sprinted across the muddy, wet ground towards the canal. The sky rumbled above them when they reached the edge of the waterway, the air heavy with the scent of impending rain.

Dan scanned the dark waters, flashing his light from side to side, but saw no sign of a boat. All he could sense — more than through his vision in the darkness — were the swaying tree branches being thrashed by the storm.

"I hate to say it, buddy, but you were wrong," Paul said. "There's gotta be another road down here somewhere you didn't know about. Dietz and everybody left by a car."

Dan shot his brother a sharp glance, grunting a frustrated response. He had been so sure of this escape route. But the canal lay empty and mocking before them, devoid of any signs of a vessel. If Dietz had escaped by car, there would be no way of getting Andrew back.

"Shh!" Dan suddenly raised a hand, his head cocked to one side like a hunting dog catching a scent. "Listen!"

"To what?" Jake asked.

"Just shut up and listen!" Dan snapped.

Jake's complaint died on his lips. The three stood still, all straining their ears. For a long moment, there was only the whooshing of the wind in the trees and water dripping from the leaves. Then it came, faint but unmistakable: the distant thrumming of an engine.

"Up the canal." Dan pointed to where the sound came from. "Hear that?"

"Yeah, I got it." Jake nodded his head.

"Me too." Paul listened to the deep throbbing a few seconds longer. "And that doesn't sound like a motor for a little skiff. Probably something bigger, like a cabin cruiser."

"I'll bet Dietz is running with no lights, as not to draw attention to himself," Dan said. "Because of that and the weather, they're traveling slow, too."

"How can they see where they're going with no light?" Jake asked.

"This canal is straight as an arrow. Just get the boat in the middle and hold it on that course," Dan said.

"Okay, but where are they going? The river's in the opposite direction, isn't it?" Paul jerked his thumb over his shoulder.

Dan aimed his flashlight on the stone edges of the waterway where the underbrush hung over and met the water. "It's too narrow for a vessel bigger than a rowboat to turn around here. They're heading for the lake to circle back towards the river."

"So they are going to have to cruise past here again," Paul said.

"Then what do we do? Wish them 'have a delightful trip' as they float by?" Irritation laced Jake's voice.

"No, we stop them," Dan said.

Jake shuffled his feet uneasily. "So we get help from the next estate over, is that it? I'll —"

"That will take too much time," Dan cut him off, his mind sorting through ideas. The sound of the engine acted like a ticking clock in his ears. "By the time anyone gets here, Dietz and company will be long gone. As will Andrew."

"What is the plan then, Danny boy?" Paul asked. "We can't exactly swim out there and ask them politely to stop."

"Give me a second." Dan tapped an index finger against his lips as he thought. After a few moments, he smiled, and said simply, "We'll catch a boat."

"Excuse me? How do you catch a boat?" Paul blinked.

"With a net, of course. What else?" Dan slapped the back of his hand on his brother's arm. "Come on."

Dan took the lead as the three scrambled their way up the slope, dodging puddles and struggling to keep their footing on the slick leaves. They finally arrived at the tennis court.

"Take that down," Dan said, waving his flashlight beam at the tennis net. Without hesitation, Paul and Jake moved to obey. They worked quickly, releasing the tension on the cables and gathering the damp mesh into their arms. "Back to the canal." Dan was already halfway out of the court.

Paul and Jake brought up the rear, hauling the weighted net. Once they reached the edge of the canal, they dropped the heavy burden onto the ground.

"Okay, I'll bite. Now what?" Paul gasped as he caught his breath.

Dan pushed the bundle resting in the mud with one foot. "We'll stretch this across the canal, underwater. When the boat passes, we let go. The net will snag the propellers. With any luck." He handed his flashlight to Jake and began to unbutton his shirt.

"What are you going to do? Get into the water? During a thunderstorm?" Jake waved his hand at the sky as thunder rolled overhead.

"That's the general idea, yes," Dan stripped to the waist. He dropped to one knee to start untying his sneakers.

"You're nuts!" Jake cried.

"I've been telling him that for years," Paul said with a half-smile as he gave Jake his flashlight as well, "but it hasn't done any good." His tee shirt joined Dan's on the ground, followed by his glasses. He started to loosen his shoelaces.

"You're screwy! You're both screwy!" Jake stared at them in disbelief. "I don't believe you guys." He hesitated only a moment longer before pulling off his shirt as well. In a few minutes, the three stood, wearing nothing but their jeans.

"Time to snag a boat." Dan pointed to the net. "Paul, you can grab one end and carry it to the opposite side. The metal cable will weigh it down in the water. The canal is only about five feet deep, so walk the netting out, heading towards the lake. I'll do the same over here. "

"Okay." Paul picked up a corner of the net. "What next?"

"Lie down on the other bank, but stay hidden under some brush. Keep your grip on the mesh, but allow it to sink into the water, an arm's length down. Its color is black, so they won't notice it floating below," Dan said. "When the boat approaches, slowly bring the net back up to the surface. Let it drag it along the bottom of the hull. The propeller should catch it and get tangled in the webbing."

"What do we do after it stops?" Jake asked.

Paul spoke up. "Jake, that's where you and I come in. I'll bet their first move will be trying to free the prop. I mean, the boat is their only way out of here. When they get into the drink to fix it, we'll be ready for them. My brother can handle himself in a fight — well, sort of, I've given him pointers — but we're the trained boxers. Stick with Dan and then join me for some fun."

Jake nodded.

Paul picked up one end of the net. "Okay, here I go." He climbed into the canal and waded to the other side. The webbing unfurled and splashed into the water. His voice came through the night. "I'm here!"

Dan hopped in next and shivered at the icy temperature. "Go!" The wet strands of the mesh bit into his palms as Dan took a few steps forward. "That's good. Now get in position."

He scrambled out and lay flat on the damp ground, near a clump of bushes. Splashing came from across the canal as Paul climbed out.

Carefully, Dan lowered the end of the net he held, his arm submerged in the frigid water. He called out to his brother. "Ready?"

"All set!" came the reply.

Jake got down next to Dan and grabbed another section of the net. The trap was ready to be sprung.

The rain began to fall again, at first gentle and then pounding down. Dan was wet, cold, and miserable. He was starting to lose feeling in his fingers. Hours seemed to pass before he suddenly snapped alert. The boat was coming back.

Anticipation and nerves charged the air, mixing with the electric smell of ozone. Dan and Jake stayed low, their breaths shallow as they became part of the scenery itself—predators lying in wait.

The pulsing of the engine grew louder, a menacing purr that sliced through the patter of raindrops on the canal's surface. Traveling down the center of the canal, the black mass of the cruiser materialized out of the darkness. A burst of lightning lit up the night, casting a pale glow on the cruiser as it cut through the choppy waters. Mac and Gus stood at the wheel. Against the backdrop of storm-tossed trees and blowing leaves, the craft appeared like a ghostly Flying Dutchman.

"Here it comes," Dan said to himself, tightening his grip on the netting.

The bow sliced past his position. Dan and Jake pulled up the net. It vibrated as the bottom of the cruiser's hull slid over it. Any second, the propeller will be in the right place...

The net suddenly snapped out of Dan and Jake's hands. A loud, high-pitched grinding sound filled the air, a shrieking protest from the engine. The once steady rumble became strained and irregular. The water around the stern churned and bubbled, with swirling eddies forming in its wake. The boat's forward motion, under its own power, stopped, and it just drifted.

Quietly, Dan and Jake slipped into the canal, staying low and only showing their noses above the surface. Paul was doing the same thing nearby, and Dan could hear him moving about.

Water lapped the cruiser's hull, the defeated engine's hum completely silenced. The rain fell in earnest now, a drumming chorus adding to the night's chaos. On deck, Dietz emerged from the cabin, his silhouette harsh against the dim interior light.

"What's going on?" he barked.

"Something's fouled the prop," Mac shouted back. "We're lucky it didn't take the bottom out."

"Then get down there and take care of it!" Dietz ordered. "Andrew's just come to. I think he'll talk after a little more persuasion. Make that repair fast! We have a schedule to keep!" He disappeared inside, slamming the cabin door.

"Him and his schedules," Gus groused. "You heard him, Mac. There's the knife."

"How am I supposed to free the propeller in the dark? Hold a light in one hand and cut with the other?" Mac protested. "You're coming in with me, pal."

"Alright, alright. Cut your bellyaching," Gus spat back. "Let's get this over with."

With Gus gripping a flashlight, Mac took up a knife, and both men entered the water. Dan moved Jake out of sight under the cover of some bush branches hanging over the edge of the canal. When Gus and Mac got to the boat's stern, Dan tapped Jake on the shoulder. He pointed down then to the two working on the propeller. Jake nodded.

The boys silently submerged themselves and swam behind Gus. As they reached him, Dan emerged first, grabbing onto Gus's sturdy shoulders. In one swift motion, he jumped up as he pushed down, shoving Gus underwater. The commotion of bubbles from Gus' struggle created a chaotic cloud under the water as he fought to resurface.

Paul came up in back of Mac and grabbed his upper arm. He spun him around and threw a punch, connecting with Mac. The burly man was resilient, shaking off the blow. His grip tightened on the handle of his blade as he lunged at Paul.

Stumbling back, Paul caught Mac's wrist with both hands, stopping the knife just inches from his chest. The water churned and splashed as they grappled, fighting to keep their feet from slipping on the slick bottom of the canal.

Gus finally broke through the surface, gasping for breath. Jake popped up in front of him and threw a punch. It landed on Gus' jaw, causing him to flounder backward into Dan. Recovering, Gus swung the flashlight at Jake, grazing the side of his head as he tried to dodge out of the way.

Mac yanked a handful of Paul's hair backward, pulling Paul off balance. Mac was stronger and backed Paul to the side of the canal, bending him over the edge. The sharp point of the knife inched dangerously close to Paul's skin.

Dan grabbed Gus' arm before he could land another blow. His other arm snaked around Gus's neck, securing a chokehold.

"Finish this, Jake!" Dan called out.

And Jake did, delivering another right cross followed by a left. Gus went limp.

"I'll take him ashore, then I'm going on board," Dan panted, dragging Gus' bulk toward the bank. "Help Paul!"

Jake thrashed through the water towards Paul. He aimed two quick rabbit punches at Mac's kidneys, causing him to flinch and loosen his grip on the knife. Paul released Mac's knife hand and landed a powerful right at his temple, sending him stumbling to the side. The weapon splashed into the canal.

Paul and Jake joined forces, unleashing a barrage of blows on Mac as if he were a punching bag. Despite his attempts to strike back, Mac couldn't stand up to their assault and eventually raised his hands in surrender.

"That really wasn't fair. Two against one," Paul said.

Jake shrugged. "There ain't no ref in a street fight."

Paul wrenched Mac's arms behind him. "Come on, move. It's time to join your pal."

The two started pushing Gus to the far side of the canal.

Dan climbed out of the water, grunting as he pulled Gus onto dry land. With the belt stripped from Gus's waist, Dan worked quickly, tying the unconscious man's hands in the back of him and the tree. The rain plastered Dan's hair to his forehead. He jumped back into the water and waded to the boat, climbing onboard.

"What's going on out there? What's taking so long?" Dietz bellowed from the cabin. "Answer me!"

Dan sprinted to the cockpit and took a position next to the door. Dietz emerged from the low entrance and climbed the short ladder to the deck. Dan launched himself at Dietz, crashing into him with full force and sending both down. They slid across the slick surface, wrestling, and trading punches.

The storm raged above, thunder clapping and lightning illuminating the scene with garish flashes. Dan twisted his body around and managed to get on top of Dietz, throwing an unanticipated right hook that connected with Dietz's chin. Reacting fast, Dietz pushed against the slippery deck with his shoes and used the momentum to roll over, reversing their positions. His fist shot out towards Dan's face, who barely dodged it by twisting his head sideways.

Dan bucked Dietz off and rolled over to a coiled rope lying nearby. Getting up, he swung the rope in front of him like a pendulum.

Dietz charged and Dan whipped the rope forward, tangling Dietz' legs. The pudgy man tripped and fell flat on his face onto the deck with an almost comical grunt. Dan dove at Dietz and locked his arms behind his back, yanking him to his feet.

"Paul! Jake! Get ready!" Dan called. "Here's another one!"

"Standing by!"

Dan shoved Dietz overboard. Splashing arose from the canal like the feeding frenzy of piranha fish.

"Got him!" Paul said back after a minute. "We'll take him to the others!"

Dan descended the ladder and entered the poorly lit cabin, dripping water. The stale air of the space was dense as he scanned the small interior. Andrew was tied up and gagged on one bunk.

"Andrew!" Dan rushed over and untied the captive. As the last knot came loose, Andrew sat up, pulling out the gag. He rubbed at his wrists.

"Thank you," Andrew said with his usual politeness, as though being offered a second serving of coffee. "I was wondering if anyone would come."

Dan took a seat on the opposite bunk. "Okay, Andrew, what's the scoop? Are you blackmailing Dietz?"

"Of course not," Andrew replied. "But he thought I was."

"Because..." Dan probed.

Andrew's expression darkened. "Dietz says he began to receive anonymous letters. The writer claimed he or she had information about my father's..." His voice wavered slightly, "... troubles."

"About not turning in the gold as per the Roosevelt Executive Order," Dan said. Andrew looked up. "I'm guessing that was the reason for the indictment."

Andrew nodded. "I don't talk about it because... I know this doesn't say much for me, but I got embarrassed about it. The letters said copies of documents existed that would prove Dietz had set up the whole thing. Framed my father. That he had intentionally held back some of the gold, then was also the person who tipped the Treasury Department about the missing amount."

"To get your father out of the way, so he could take over," Dan said.

"Yes. Dietz played the long game, meticulous in his planning. He became indispensable to the business over the years, handling all the paperwork. My father trusted him completely." Andrew stared at the deck. "More lucrative government contracts started coming in as war with Germany seemed inevitable. The foundry was booming. Dietz then made his move to get my father out. If only I had…" His voice trailed off in regret.

"But you were getting these same letters, too, weren't you?"

"Not as blackmail. The offer was for documents that would clear my father's name while proving Dietz guilty. I didn't know he was receiving them, too, until… later." Andrew looked at Dan. "How did you get your hands on those copies? You must have searched my room."

"I, ah, did," Dan said with an apologetic smile. "I got a tip."

"From whom?"

"I don't know." Dan shrugged.

"But I never received those ledger sheets," Andrew said. "Dietz had me then."

Dan shrugged. "They were in your room. We'll have to put that in the 'unknown' pile for now. How did Dietz kidnap you?"

"I received a note telling me to meet somebody at the center of the maze," Andrew answered.

"And you thought it would be the mysterious letter writer," Dan said.

Andrew nodded. "Instead, it was those goons — Gus and Mac — waiting for me. They knocked me out with something soaked in a cloth. When I woke up, I was tied, gagged, and blindfolded in the trunk of a car. After being driven around for what I think was several hours, I was brought to a house and bound to a chair. Gus and Mac took turns questioning me."

"And Dietz was there?"

"Probably directing the whole thing. Mac and Gus aren't smart enough to think up those questions they asked. I sensed that another person was present, but I still had the blindfold on and couldn't be sure. They only took it off when I was taken to the dungeon."

"Were you held in the gardener's cottage?"

"Yes. The long drive was a ruse to make me think I was someplace else," Andrew said. "When I saw the person in the monk costume tonight, I knew it was certain Dietz was behind this. He doesn't have much imagination."

"Why not just tell him you were getting the same letters?" Dan asked, confusion lacing his words.

"You heard him. He convinced himself I'm the one in back of it all," Andrew said. "Dietz is like a dog with a bone. Once he latches onto an idea, there's no shaking it off. He wouldn't have believed me... especially since he already pegged me as the culprit. If I told him I also had received letters, he'd assume I knew more than I actually did. So I decided playing dumb was the only way to go."

Andrew shook his head. He went on in a quieter voice. "And there's something more. Dietz never thought much of me. You heard him. I don't think he's alone in his opinion. Maybe... maybe it was time for him and everybody to see that I am capable of more than they give me credit for. I can stand up for things. And against things. Perhaps it was time for me to prove it to myself, too."

Before Dan could respond, Paul came into the cabin, dripping with water. "Dan, I see lights—red and blue — flashing through the trees. It must be the cops. Jake's gone to bring them down."

"Good," Dan nodded, standing up. "Oh, Andrew, this is my brother, Paul."

Andrew stood and extended this hand. "I am pleased to make your acquaintance."

Paul was a little surprised at the formality. He shook Andrew's hand. "Ah, yeah, thanks. Me too."

"Let's get you out of here and sort this mess out once and for all," Dan said.

Andrew glanced between Dan and Paul. "You two are identical. Now I recognize your name. The Case twins. I read about you both in the paper a few months ago."

Dan grinned. "That's us. Right now, we need to get topside and wait for the police. Everybody is going to have to make statements."

Chapter Seventeen

The afternoon light poured through the French windows two weeks later, casting a gentle glow on the polished mahogany desk where Mrs. Maitland sat. Dan, Paul, and Jake, dressed in their suits, stood attentively before her. She finished signing another check and pulled it from the register.

"Paul and Jake, please accept this as a token of my thanks," Mrs. Maitland said as she extended checks toward them. "For your assistance in rescuing Andrew — $400 each."

Jake and Paul accepted their rewards with grins.

"And Daniel," she continued, turning her gaze towards him with an appreciative smile, "I've added the same amount to your commission for the beautiful painting I am sure you have completed."

"Thank you, Mrs. Maitland," the three boys said in unison, almost like a trained singing trio.

"You are all most welcome. You all deserve it," Mrs. Maitland said as she returned the checkbook to the top drawer. "I must say, the ordeal has altered Andrew. My lawyer thinks the family will regain control of the foundry. Andrew says he's determined to become more involved with the business. He's going to go in next week. It's heartening to see."

Mrs. Maitland leaned back in her chair, regarding Jake. "And Jake, have you given any thought to my proposal? Part-time chauffeur until graduation — I expect nothing less than completion, of course — then full-time thereafter. Your mother could stay in the gardener's cottage. And once we secure the foundry again, I'm certain there will be a position for her in the office."

Jake's response came quick, his eagerness barely contained. "You bet! That'll be swell!"

Dan, standing next to Jake, gave him a discrete kick to the side of his ankle.

"Yes, ma'am, I'd like that very much." Jake corrected. "May I use the phone to tell her?"

"Certainly." Mrs. Maitland gestured toward the hall. "The telephone is at your disposal."

With a buoyant stride, Jake excused himself. In a few moments, his voice boomed in from the hallway. "Hey, Ma! Guess what! We can scram out of that dump!"

Mrs. Maitland nodded toward Jake's voice with a smile. "A nice young man, if a trifle rough around the edges. I'm sure Andrew will take him under his wing. Maybe even teach him tennis." She stood and glanced at Dan with a twinkle in her eye. "Once we purchase a new net. And Paul, I look forward to your designs for the front flowerbeds."

Paul grinned. "I can't wait to start."

"Of course, Daniel, I'm most excited to see your completed work." Mrs. Maitland gestured to the door. "I have a particular interest in how you captured Max and Brutus' fierce, brutal, animalistic nature."

"It was tricky," Dan said in complete honesty. "I hope you like it."

"Well, let us join the others for the unveiling," Mrs. Maitland said. "Simply everybody is there! Your art teacher, my bridge clue, even Lang! Simply everybody!"

The twins followed Mrs. Maitland into the living room where the reception was taking place. An easel stood in front of the fireplace, the painting hidden under a red cloth. The room buzzed with the murmur of conversations and the clink of fine china on a sideboard laden with hors d'oeuvres. Mrs. Danner, her hair impeccably coiffed, presided over the spread with the aplomb of a general overseeing troops. Mrs. Maitland left the boys to join the members of her bridge and women's club. They mingled among the gathering, their laughter tinkling through the air like wind chimes.

Dan's art teacher, Miss Cohen, was also in the group. She smiled at Dan as he came in. Standing next to the fireplace, Lang glowered, not happy to be there and making sure everybody knew it. Andrew sprawled in a chair, wearing his usual uninterested expression. He held a leash in both hands, keeping the rambunctious Max and Brutus at bay.

"He's changed?" Paul said out of the corner of his mouth.

Dan glanced toward Andrew, who returned a nod and half-smile. "He looks marginally less bored."

"Where's Mom?" Paul scanned the room, his brow knitting as he failed to locate their mother among the guests.

"Out on the terrace." Dan tilted his head toward the open French windows. Their mother and Steve stood next to one other, gazing out over the estate.

"He's too close to her," Paul fumed.

"They're interested in each other, that's all," Dan said, his tone gentle but firm.

"I can see that," Paul snapped back. "I got eyes, don't I?"

Dan placed a reassuring hand on Paul's shoulder. "Paul, it's been three years since Dad was killed. Nothing can replace him in all our hearts—yours, mine, and especially Mom's. But doesn't she deserve another chance at happiness?"

"Of course she does," Paul conceded, the fight leaving his voice. He added quietly. "Doesn't make it any easier, though."

"I know that, buddy. Don't I know that," Dan said.

"Speaking of difficult..." Paul's tone shifted as he inclined his head towards Donna, talking and laughing with Romero. Dan followed his brother's gaze, sputtering at the sight.

"Life's full of tough spots," Paul nudged Dan with his elbow. "Isn't it, my dear brother?"

Dan and Paul navigated through the sea of guests, their polished shoes clicking on the hardwood floor. The soft murmur of conversations mingled with the clinking of glasses. As they reached

Donna and Betty, Romero — his dark eyes flickering to Dan — murmured an excuse and drifted away in search of coffee.

Donna folded her arms and arched one eyebrow at Dan. "Daniel Case, you liar! He isn't married, and he doesn't have a bunch of kids. No dog or canary, either." With a playful slap at Dan's arm, she smiled at him. "Now don't get jealous, handsome. Mr. Romero — Ricardo to his friends —," she pointed to herself, "has a fiancée, and their wedding is in June. He said this was one knot Paul couldn't cut. Oh, and he promised he'd send us invitations."

"Oh, really?" Dan said, relieved. "I need to give him my congratulations."

"I still can't believe Andrew was tucked away in the gardener's cottage all the time," Betty said. "Right under everybody's noses!"

"You could say hidden in plain sight," Dan remarked.

"Yeah, like that story by Edgar Allan Poe," Paul chimed in. "'The Postponed Letter,' it was called."

"'Purloined'," Dan, Betty, and Donna said as one.

Paul shrugged. "Yeah, that too."

As if on cue, Mrs. Case and Steve returned from the terrace. Dan and Paul proudly displayed their checks to their mother.

Mrs. Case hugged each one of them. "I'm so proud of you two. Your father would have been, too."

Dan and Paul grinned. Steve stuck out his hand.

"You both did a great job," he said, shaking the twin's hands.

"Even if I didn't leave the investigation to you?" Dan asked with a smile.

Steve winked. "We'll just let that lie for the time being."

"This is enough money to buy that used Studebaker truck on Waxton's lot, don't you think?" Paul said as he slipped the check into his wallet. "If I get it, I can start my business after I graduate." He spread his hands wide as he proclaimed the name. "Case Landscaping Service — Transforming Yards, One Lawn at a Time. How does that sound? I'll have my artistic brother paint that on the doors."

"Sure," Dan said. "I'll give you a discount off my usual fee."

Paul pretended to be a tough guy and poked his twin in the chest with his index finger. "You'll do it for free there, pal."

"Oh, don't beat me again, kind sir!" Dan pleaded with folded hands.

The group laughed. Dan fidgeted with the check in his hand. "Still, there's something off about this whole thing," he said, almost to himself. "It's not finished."

Donna turned to Betty. "We've heard that before."

"Well, it's true." Dan slipped the check into his wallet. "Something's not right."

"What do you mean?" Steve took a step closer to Dan.

"Andrew was Dietz's captive, right?" Donna asked.

"Sure, that is clear. Dietz kidnapped him," Dan answered, nodding. "But there's more to it... It doesn't all add up. You know, I think Dietz was as much a victim as Andrew."

"What?" Steve exclaimed.

"Someone else pulled the strings. And may still do it," Dan said. "A Mr. X behind the scenes."

"It's always 'Mr. X,' isn't it?" Paul said with a wry grin. He leaned over to Betty. "Every mystery story known to man has a Mr. X."

"Okay, okay," Dan replied, a flash of irritation in his eyes. "Let's call him the 'Mysterious Mr. M,' then. Does that meet with your approval?" He glanced at Paul, who paused, considering, before giving a silent nod of agreement.

"Fine. Now we've got that settled... the Mysterious Mr. M was the mastermind behind everything. He ran the show, hidden in back of the curtain, moving people like chess pieces," Dan went on, firm with conviction. "I've been thinking about it all week, and I have a feeling I know who it is."

Paul couldn't contain himself. His loud voice cut through the conversation like an air-raid siren. "You know who's behind this whole setup?"

"Sheesh, Paul. Why not use a megaphone the next time?" Dan complained.

Dan realized the room had fallen silent. He glanced over his shoulder. Every pair of eyes in the place was fixed on him. It was like when the new sheriff in town steps onto a saloon full of bad guys in a Western movie.

Donna gave Dan a gentle nudge. She waved her hand toward the rest of the people in the living room. "The floor is yours, handsome."

Dan took a steadying breath, ready to unravel the mystery that had entwined the Maitland mansion. The anticipation in the air was electric, and amid the sea of expectant faces, he knew it was time to bare the facts as he saw it.

He stepped to the center of the room, all sound drained out of the room. Every eye was upon him as though he were about to pull off a grand magic trick... or fall flat on his face. He cleared his throat.

"Let's start with some background," Dan began, his voice trembling a little from nerves. "Mr. Amos Maitland was a man of contradictions. Mrs. Danner told me he was brilliant at the nuts-and-bolts of running the foundry, but became stressed by the chaos of paperwork. His anxiety and worry over it gnawed at him enough to give him a peptic ulcer."

Mrs. Maitland and Mrs. Danner both nodded in agreement. Dan took a moment to let the image sink in before continuing with more confidence. "Then came Tony Dietz—organized, reliable, just who Mr. Maitland needed. His meticulous nature was the perfect counter to Mr. Maitland's disorganization. Dietz was brought on to handle the business's administration and eventually moved into a full partnership." Dan scanned the audience, paying attention to their reactions as he wove together his tale. "But little did Mr. Maitland understand, Dietz had bigger ambitions than just being a partner. He wanted the entire foundry for his own."

Dan took a couple of steps forward. "In 1933, President Roosevelt's executive order made it illegal for individuals to own gold. Dietz reassured Mr. Maitland he would take care of the situation, and he did... sort of. Trusting Dietz, Mr. Maitland did not think to check for himself. That turned out to be a huge mistake. While

Dietz surrendered some of Mr. Maitland's gold to the authorities, claiming it was all there was, he secreted some away. But not for profit. Gold was to become Dietz's weapon. He planned to hold on to it until it was right to use it for his own purposes. And he was willing to wait as long as necessary."

The room remained hushed, hanging on Dan's every word. He could feel the tension mounting like static in the air, ready to snap.

"September 1939 came, and with it, Hitler's invasion of Poland. The world took a sharp turn towards global warfare," Dan said. "Dietz could see what was coming — more military contracts for the foundry, an influx of money from a war-driven economy. He decided it was time to make his move, get Mr. Maitland out of the picture, and keep all the profits for himself. Dietz made an anonymous tip to the US Treasury Department about Mr. Maitland's remaining gold.

When he heard he was under investigation from the government, Mr. Maitland panicked. Dietz, ever the serpent, whispered fear into his ear, convincing him fleeing the US was his only way to avoid prison. He suggested Argentina since that country doesn't have an extradition treaty with the US. Am I right?" Dan turned to Romero, who confirmed with a nod. "Mr. Maitland fled, leaving Dietz to claim his prize: the foundry. He squeezed out every dime during the chaos of war."

Dan's gaze swept over everybody in the room. "Dietz thought he had executed the perfect crime," he went on, his voice low and deliberate. "But then, six months ago, letters began to arrive. Blackmail. This Mysterious Mr. M claimed he or she had possession of the documents Dietz kept so meticulously. Dietz discovered they had indeed been stolen. Papers showing the gold transfer, and maybe some hanky-panky with the government contracts."

Dan turned to Romero. "The Pentagon may want to perform an audit, by the way. To Dietz, these very papers could mean a prison sentence for him. At the same time, Andrew received similar messages, offering the same documents for sale. Ones which would clear his father and prove the frame-up. Andrew even took a trip to Argentina to talk over the situation with Mr. Maitland, telling his mother he was going to Palm Springs."

"Andrew, is that true?" Mrs. Maitland accused. Andrew returned a brief nod. "We'll discuss the matter later. Please continue, Daniel."

Donna's brow wrinkled in confusion. "Why send letters to both Dietz and Andrew?"

"Simple," Mrs. Case explained. "The anonymous letter writer wanted them at each other's throats, hoping to start a bidding war."

"Exactly, but the plan went haywire," Dan said. "Dietz became convinced somehow Andrew was behind the scheme and had hidden the documents in this house. Disguised as the monk, he searched the property. When that failed, he kidnapped Andrew, making it appear Andrew had taken a trip to California. Then Dietz attempted to force Andrew through various means to disclose the location of those papers. Despite the pressure and, uh, unpleasant methods used, Andrew refused to say anything."

Mrs. Maitland gasped, one hand coming to her mouth, and looked at Andrew. Andrew shrugged, but there was a glint of pride in his eyes.

"What was Dietz going to do with Andrew?" asked Betty.

Dan gestured toward the Maitland son to explain.

"He made an arrangement with the captain of a tramp steamer," Andrew said. "I was going to be dispatched on a long ocean voyage, to be put off on a small, sparsely populated Pacific island. It would have taken me months to arrange a passage home. He was smuggling me to the ship when Dan and his friends freed me."

"And the time Andrew was out of the way would have given Dietz time to sell the foundry, pocket the cash, and perhaps follow Mr. Maitland's footsteps to South America," Dan said.

"So what about the Mysterious Mr. M? The kidnapping must have upset his plans," Steve asked.

"It did," Dan said. "It wasn't about money anymore. So the Mysterious Mr. M's motive changed."

"Into what?" asked Romero.

Dan shook his head. "I'm still not sure. Anyway, I found myself an unwitting player in the game in the new plot. I received notes that led me to clues to the truth about Andrew's disappearance while Dietz and his men did everything they could to interfere with me. They listened in on my phone calls and stole any clues I found, including a ledger page from the documents. But since it was an exact copy of the one sent to Dietz, it's possible the Mysterious Mr. M didn't actually have a full set of pages as he claimed, only just a few."

The room was silent. Donna broke it with her question: "Who is this Mysterious Mr. M?"

"I've been using 'Mr.' because it's easier than saying 'Mr., Mrs. or Miss.' all the time. But it could be any of the three." Dan's eyes swept over each person in the room. He was relaxing now, almost as though he was a detective hero in one of the Agatha Christie mysteries he consumed. "And the Mysterious Mr. M is in this room."

A ripple of unease spread through the partygoers. Dan continued, aware of the shift in the atmosphere. "Mystery stories are full of red herrings, and suspects. We know the Mysterious Mr. M has to be a member of the household since he had access to the property. But who is it? Take Mrs. Maitland," he said, walking to the matriarch. "Often, the most affable can be masking a nefarious heart. Plus, her typewriter produced the notes sent to me."

Mrs. Maitland stiffened, her eyes darting around the room nervously.

"Or it may be Andrew," Dan went on, taking a position in front of the younger Maitland. "It wouldn't be unheard of for a villain to pretend to be the victim, to throw suspicion off their scent."

Andrew's expression didn't change.

Dan pressed on, "And let's not overlook the household staff." He locked his eyes toward Romero, who met his gaze unflinchingly. "It could be somebody from the government. Even though working undercover as a chauffeur, why not exploit privileged information for personal gain?"

"We also have Mrs. Danner." He went to the housekeeper stationed behind the hors d'oeuvres table and picked up a deviled egg. "Could a long-time employee decide to secure a comfortable future by illicit means?" He smiled at her as he took a bite of the egg. Mrs. Danner stood straight and looked him dead in the eye. One of her hands moved to a knife. "Even if she is a wonderful cook."

Dan finished the egg as he walked to Lang. "Of course, there's always that terrible cliché in mystery stories — the butler did it." A brief smile danced on his lips before his face grew somber once more. "But is it also true about the gardener?"

He took a step forward and reached out to Lang in one fluid motion. He grabbed onto what had been thought to be a wild mop of hair and gave it a sharp tug. The wig slipped off, exposing a shiny bald head underneath. Dan held the toupee up like a flag, but his moment of triumph was short-lived.

"Lang, our gardener?" Mrs. Maitland's voice was laced with confusion as she peered at the man who had tended her roses and trimmed her hedges.

Paul stepped forward and pointed at Lang. "That guy's no gardener. I do landscaping, and you're lucky anything is still alive on this place with him attending to it."

"Then who is he?" Mrs. Maitland leaned forward a little to squint at Lang.

"You don't know?" Dan asked.

"Why, no, I don't," she shrugged.

"This is not Mr. Maitland, in disguise?" Dan hoped. He added lamely, "After some plastic surgery, maybe…"

"Of course not! I'd know my own husband!" Mrs. Maitland huffed with a mix of indignation and certainty.

"Oh." Dan's response was almost sheepish, an anticlimactic murmur lost in the sudden tension gripping the room.

Lang's voice scratched with a bitter edge, his voice rang heavy with resentment. "Of course, she wouldn't know. I worked on the foundry floor for twenty years. Twenty long, hot, hard years. When I retired, all I got was this gold watch." He spat the words out as if they were poison, his free hand reaching to touch the timepiece. "Two decades, every single day, I worked myself to the bone, making Maitland and Dietz richer. They sat up in their cushy offices, profiting off the sweat of my labor, taking more than their fair share."

Andrew's emotions were as controlled as ever as he responded. "Now listen… I understand it's easy to see this as unfair, but building and running a business is no simple task. The risks and responsibilities fell on my father's shoulders. He was on the hook to maintain the place, to make sure there was still a job for everyone who relied on it. The foundry didn't come out of nowhere. It required significant investment, planning, and sleepless nights to keep everything afloat."

"Well said, Andrew," Mrs. Maitland approved with a nod.

Lang's lips parted, and when he spoke, his voice was the sound of grinding gears, the mechanical rasp of a lifetime of labor. "But it's the workers' hands that made it run. Without us, the foundry wouldn't produce a single rivet. You may think you're entitled to the fruits of our labor just because you own the building, but ownership doesn't make you the one who deserves all the profits. It's the workers who slave on the floor, not the ones sitting in the office, far from the noise, the heat, and the danger."

Mrs. Maitland, her voice steady yet laced with an undercurrent of frustration, spoke. "Don't be melodramatic. Hardly slaves. My husband always paid the workers the best wages in the area and provided benefits as well."

Lang's lips twisted into a sneer. "Not enough. One day soon, the proletariat will overthrow this system of exploitation. You'll see — we deserve more."

Steve stepped forward. "No more speeches, everybody. Lang, it's time you come with me."

Without warning, Lang's hand shot out, wrapping around Dan's throat with a vice-like grip. The cold, hard circle of a gun barrel pressed against Dan's temple, a silent but unmistakable threat that turned the air in the living room to ice.

"One move from anyone," Lang snarled, "and the bright boy here gets it."

Chapter Eighteen

Dan's heartbeat thundered in his ears, a staccato rhythm that seemed to echo the cold stillness of the room. He breathed in shallow drafts, and he fought to keep his wits about him, aware that any sudden movement could be his last. Lang's hand was steady, the gun resting on Dan's temple.

The silence was total, the collective breath of the onlookers held tight in their throats. Everybody was still making the room as static as a wax museum exhibit. The tension wrapped around everybody and everything, time slowing until each second ticked off in an eternity.

Lang jerked his head towards the French door. "Now, bright boy and I are going out that door. Nobody moves."

The icy metal of the barrel pressed against Dan's head, a contrast to the beads of sweat forming on his forehead. With every step forward, the pressure increased, his heart racing in fear.

One foot, two feet, three feet... the pair slowly crossed the room. They neared the chair where Andrew sat.

He dropped the leashes of Max and Brutus.

The two Great Danes scrambled across the short distance, leaping onto Dan and Lang with all their heft. The impact sent all of them crashing to the floor, tangled in limbs, paws, and tails. Lang's grip on the gun loosened, and it slipped out of his hand, skidding along the smooth wood floors.

One of Mrs. Maitland's bridge club members picked it up. "I've got it! I've got it! What do I do with it now?" she wailed.

Flying across the room, Paul launched himself at Lang, pinning him down. Jake was right behind, adding his weight to the restraint. Romero and Steve surged forward, sorting out the human and canine melee with practiced ease. Steve snapped handcuffs around Lang's wrists, clicking them shut.

Mrs. Case snatched the gun from the woman. "Here. Better give that to me before you hurt somebody."

Steve's grip on Lang's arm was tight as he hauled the cuffed man to his feet, but Lang was not to be so easily subdued. His voice, a ragged blend of triumph and madness, echoed through the room as he faced everybody in the room with wild eyes.

"Bright boy here got one thing wrong," Lang said, tilting his head in Dan's direction, growing louder with each word. "He said I didn't have all the papers. I do. All of them. The whole lot." A pause for effect, a sneer curling his lip. "I befriended Ollie the janitor and 'helped him' clean the plant. Nice guy that I am. I used his passkeys to get into the offices, and I searched the files and found Dietz' records. Detailed notes on how he didn't turn in all the gold to the government like he said he did. He wrote it all down, in neat, tidy little columns. The fool! So I took them.

Dietz got rid of Maitland, and now I've gotten rid of Dietz! Dietz will be in prison, and Maitland will never be able to return home! Do you think Dietz will confess what he did? Ha! And the papers are safe! They're needed to clear Maitland, and they sit right in front of your stupid noses, and you'll never find them. Never! You can tear down this whole house and it will do no good! I ruined both of them! I've won! I've won!"

Laughter bubbled up from his throat, unhinged and resonant, filling the room as Steve dragged him out, his mirth a fading echo down the corridor.

Everybody rushed up to Dan, enveloping him in a chaotic embrace. His mother squeezed him tightly, tears streaming down her face. Donna and Betty joined the group hug. Amidst the commotion, they all kept asking the same question over and over again, "Are you alright?"

"I'm fine," he said, "thanks to my heroes."

Paul shrugged modestly. "Nobody holds a gun on my little brother. Especially not when Jake and I are around."

"Oh, you guys were great," Dan said. He reached down to the dogs. "But here are my real heroes."

Dan scratched Max and Brutus behind their ears, causing their tails to thump against the floor. He looked up at Paul and Jake with a grin on his face.

Jake pointed to Dan and spoke to Paul. "I don't believe this guy."

Paul rolled his eyes. "That's my dear brother."

Dan indicated the gun. "Ah, Mom, shouldn't you be careful with that?"

Mrs. Case glanced at the revolver. "Oh, it's fine. I've already snapped on the safety."

"Looks like you've handled one of those before," Dan said.

Holding the weapon with casual assurance, Mrs. Case gave a noncommittal shrug.

Romero brushed off his suit, his eyes studying Dan. "So how did you figure it was Lang?"

"Why, it was—" Dan began.

"Don't you dare say 'elementary, my dear Watson'," Paul lobbed in.

"A cakewalk," Dan said, with a nod of his head to his brother. "Simple process of elimination. I found out at least one of the notes I got came from Mrs. Maitland's typewriter. It's likely that all of them were typed on the same machine. So, the culprit must have had regular access to the house in order to accomplish this. That narrowed the list of possible suspects.

We know Dietz got in here since he was creeping around the place in his monk's outfit while he searched for the documents. He used Mrs. Maitland's typewriter to forge the note from Andrew about leaving for California. However, it wouldn't make sense for him to be responsible for the other notes. So somebody else was my unknown helper... and also planted those documents in Andrew's room I found. So I became curious about others in the house. For example, there was the money I found in Lang's hotel room."

"How'd you get into Lang's room?" Romero asked.

"With a key," Dan answered.

"But..." Romero sputtered.

Donna waved her hand between herself and Betty. "We played a little distraction game with the desk clerk, so Dan could steal it."

"Borrow it, Donna," Dan corrected quickly. "I just borrowed it."

Romero started to say something, but Mrs. Case intervened with a gentle touch to his arm. "Don't ask," she advised. "I find it easier that way."

The Treasury agent closed his mouth. He gestured for Dan to go on.

"Anyway," Dan continued, steering the conversation back on track, "the amount I found was a tidy sum for a gardener's salary, even by Mrs. Maitland's generous standards. It could have been some early payments from Dietz or Andrew. Plus, there was the Treasury department number Lang had scribbled down on the telephone notepad."

"You knew it off the top of your head when I asked," Paul said to Romero.

Dan nodded toward Romero. "I mean, that makes sense... you work there. You wouldn't need to write it down. But Lang did. Why? He may have become suspicious about you and was checking up. Or he called to add that tip about Maitland entering the country in disguise. The money and the phone number pointed to Lang, at least to me. Without concrete proof, though, it was just a hunch."

"What cinched it?" Jake asked.

"The day Mrs. Maitland announced her trip to New York City," Dan said. "Mrs. Danner had already gone. Romero, you were busy with the luggage, then you drove Mrs. Maitland to the train station. When I put the flashlight I bought earlier in the afternoon on my bed, no note was in the room. But after the two of you left — and neither one of you went upstairs in the meantime — there it was. And who was still on the property? Only Lang."

A silence befell them as the weight of the deduction settled. Then came a murmur of approval from the party guests. Dan was surprised for a moment. He had completely forgotten about their presence.

It was broken by Mrs. Maitland's plaintive voice, tinged with the residue of shock. "After all this commotion, I do feel quite unwell," Mrs. Maitland said. Her hands fluttered to her abdomen as if to quell the uneasiness. "Mrs. Danner, is there any milk in the house?"

"Of course, Mrs. Maitland," Mrs. Danner said, already moving towards the kitchen with a practiced efficiency.

The air in the room had barely settled from the recent excitement when Dan held up both hands and froze. He gazed through everybody as if they were mere apparitions. An idea was forming in his mind, elusive yet persistent — something dancing in shadows at the edge of understanding. "Wait... milk... purloined letter... milk... purloined letter... right in front of your nose..."

"Stand back, folks!" Paul held his arms wide, as though keeping back a crowd from a fire. "My brother has just kicked his thinking cap into high gear! Watch out for flying parts!"

"Quiet! Let me think!" Dan ordered. The idea was there, in his brain, hiding in a corner. He coaxed it out. "Come on, baby... come on…" The solution emerged into the light. He slapped his hands together as his eyes brightened and a grin spread across his lips. "Of course! I think I've got it! That's it! It has to be!" He grabbed his twin's shoulders and shook him. The words tumbled out. "Purloined letter! Purloined letter! I don't care what you people say, my dear brother! You're not stupid!"

"Hey! Who thinks I'm stupid?" Paul protested.

Pushing his way through the people, Dan dashed out of the room, Paul directly behind him. The remainder of the guests trailed in their wake.

Dan came to a stop in front of the grand portrait of Amos Maitland in the hallway. His attention was drawn towards the desk depicted in the foreground of the painting. He reached out his hand, lightly brushing against the painted the canvas desktop. "Purloined letter…"

He carefully ran his fingers along the edges of each envelope shown in the art. Under his breath, he said to himself, "No… no…" He was starting to worry he was wrong, but then —

His movements paused as he found a particular letter's image that felt rough to the touch. Moving closer, within mere inches of the image, he scrutinized the same area. He nodded. "Slight sheen…" He stepped back. "I'll need an iron, please."

"An iron? What is it?" Mrs. Danner's voice carried a note of bewilderment.

"It's a domestic appliance to take wrinkles out of clothes!" Paul said in exasperation. "My brother needs one!"

"Please fetch one for him," Mrs. Maitland said.

Mumbling to herself, Mrs. Danner bustled off to the kitchen.

"Help me with this, would you?" Dan waved Paul over, nodding towards the portrait. Together, they carefully lifted it from the hook and set it gently on the floor, leaning against the wall. Dan knelt in front of the painting, staring at it, tapping his lips with his index finger.

Mrs. Danner returned with the iron and Dan took it from her. He plugged the iron into the nearest outlet, flicked it to the lowest heat setting, and sat back on his knees.

"Revenge," Dan said. "That's what Lang's motivation evolved into when Dietz kidnapped Andrew. It was no longer just about financial gain, but it turned into a personal vendetta." He paused for a second. "What was the twist in 'The Purloined Letter'?"

Betty's reply was immediate. "The stolen letter was hidden in plain sight."

"Exactly," Dan affirmed with a nod. "Altered, yet visible to everyone. Kind of like Andrew, hidden in the cottage all along. Keep that point in mind. Here's something else, which may seem unrelated. But it's not." He glanced at the portrait. "Mr. Maitland's ulcer required him to drink milk — a soothing remedy for his stomach. But milk has also served a more arcane purpose throughout history. As invisible ink."

The iron emitted a faint hum as it reached temperature. He passed the warmed appliance over the canvas, moving slowly back and forth over the area where the letter lay on the painted desk of Amos Maitland.

"Lang wanted revenge against Mr. Maitland and Dietz. He hated both of them and what they stood for," Dan said in a quiet tone as he concentrated on his task. "Dietz is facing a kidnapping charge now. He's finished. Will he confess to framing Mr. Maitland by withholding the gold? It's uncertain. But consider the irony of Lang's brutal retaliation... the cruelness of it towards the Maitlands."

The guests remained silent. Everyone leaned in closer, eyes fixed on the painting, waiting for revelation or disappointment.

"He hid crucial evidence in plain sight, where Mrs. Maitland and Andrew would see it every day," Dan said. "Andrew told me his father bought the house with all the furnishings and art. Except for this piece. The Maitlands would look at this painting, unaware that the key to clear Mr. Maitland's name was right in front of them. In their own home. The solution to his return to this country as a free man, tantalizingly close but completely out of reach. That would weigh on the entire Maitland family... knowing that the truth was out there, somewhere, but they couldn't get their hands on it. That's why Lang said he had won."

Dan's grip on the iron was firm and precise as he waved it over the envelope painted on the canvas. A hushed gasp spread through the crowd as the heat from the iron revealed a ghostly 'B'. More characters materialized in the hidden message, one by one. "BFNB 458," he read aloud. He smiled as put down the iron, turning it off.

"Good heavens," Mrs. Maitland breathed. "What does that mean?"

"Lang said the papers were 'safe'... *in* a safe. I bet 'BFNB 458' stands for Belmont First National Bank, safe deposit box 458," Dan said, his gaze still fixed on the painting as if it might reveal more secrets. "The documents... they're in there."

Romero nodded. "I'll get a search warrant immediately."

Dan stood. Paul slapped him on the back. "Well done, my dear brother."

"I'm sorry I implicated everybody else," Dan said, "but..."

"But that's the way it's done in the books he reads," Paul finished.

Mrs. Maitland let out a long breath. "My, this has been an exciting afternoon, hasn't it? But it is not completed yet. There is more to come!" She resumed her role as the hostess. She clapped her hands like a kindergarten teacher getting the attention of her charges. "Alright, everyone," she said with a flourish, "let's return to the reason we have gathered here today. To see the unveiling of Daniel's artwork."

The atmosphere shifted from one of suspense to a buzz of anticipation. Mrs. Maitland gracefully herded the guests into the living room. They formed a semicircle around the covered painting, Dan standing to one side. Max and Brutus took their places at the front like two canine sentinels. The dogs' tails wagged in sync.

"All right, Daniel, let us proceed," Mrs. Maitland directed. "Now, everybody! Let's give our full attention to our young artist."

"Not that he hasn't been getting it all day," Paul said to his mother out of the corner of his mouth. She smiled and nodded.

Dan cleared his throat. "Well, I... um..." His words trailed off, then he flashed a sheepish smile, "I forgot what I was going to say."

"My dear brother puts the finger on a blackmailer and deduces the location of stolen documents, but can't remember a ten-word speech." Paul raised his hands helplessly as he addressed the other guests. "You see what Mom and I have to put up with?"

Dan chuckled. "It was a boring speech, anyway. I'll cut to the chase. I hope you'll all like the painting." He reached for the cloth.

With a swift motion, he pulled the fabric away, revealing the artwork beneath. He sucked in his breath. What rested on the easel was not the meticulously crafted piece he had spent countless hours perfecting. There was a moment of stunned silence as the gathered assembly took in the scene in front of them.

"Ah—" was all Dan could muster, staring in dismay at the sight before him.

The picture showed seven dogs, an assortment of breeds from German shepherd to mastiff. Each one captured was a caricature of a gambler from a bygone era, their expressions oozing with cunning and mischief. Their paws expertly held playing cards. Some clamped pipes between their teeth, while others clenched stubby cigars. On a green, felt-topped table sat discarded cards and poker chips, accompanied by half-empty beer bottles. At the forefront of the scene, a stout bulldog attempted a sly pass of an ace under the table with a sneaky paw to another bulldog, both with knowing smirks on their faces.

The first snicker bubbled up from Mrs. Case, irrepressible and infectious. It spread like wildfire, the room erupting into laughter as the absurdity hit home. Dan snapped his head from the painting and glared at Paul. His brother was attempting to keep a straight face and maintain an angelic expression at the same time. He failed.

Paul held up his hands for quiet as he stepped up to his sibling. "Sorry, ladies and gentlemen, sorry. My fault. I made a mistake and put up the wrong picture. This is Dan's *next* work of art. He's doing it for a combination pet store and saloon. Now here's his portrait of Max and Brutus."

With a dramatic gesture, Paul grabbed a corner of the poker-playing canines poster and whisked it away to reveal the true work beneath. The sound of laughter was suddenly hushed as the figures of Max and Brutus emerged into view.

With their heads held high and their powerful frames on display, the images of the Great Danes embodied a regal air as they stood against the magnificent backdrop of the Maitland Mansion. The vibrant colors of the mansion's stonework contrasted with the deep black and tan of the dog's coats. It was as if the two were meant to be there, adding an element of grandeur to the already impressive scene. Applause filled the room, a warm cascade that washed over Dan.

Dan turned to his brother. "I hate you."

Paul looked back at his twin, his smile broadening into a Cheshire cat grin.

9 781962 056083